To Gerry, who doesn't mind the tears.

NOTE TO READERS

This book, set in 1964, uses words that are no longer accepted. These words are *Negro* and *colored*, the latter specifically as it relates to people of African origin. At the time in which this book is set, these words were widely used in society and in the media. Their use in this book is for historical accuracy only and in no way implies acceptance of them today.

Chapter One

MY STORY BEGINS

TWO THINGS YOU need to know about me: I always dreamed about being a newspaper reporter, and I'm an orphan.

I was mostly raised in an orphanage, although I know from hearing one of the staff gossip about it that I had been adopted as a baby and then given up again when the childless couple who had wanted me so badly discovered that they were about to have a child of their own. The person who said that, who shall remain nameless here, said she thought that had to be the very worst, to be unwanted twice over.

The orphanage where I grew up was called the Benevolent Home for Necessitous Girls. I lived there until I couldn't stand it anymore, which happened to coincide with the age at which most girls get itchy anyway, when they think they're going to explode if they have to look at the same faces all day for another day and another day after that, when it seems as if nothing ever changes and nothing ever will, when every day is exactly the same as the one before. When you would (almost) literally give your right arm for something different to happen. There were days when I thought I would go crazy if I had to spend another sixty seconds surrounded by orphan girls and spinster women.

I know, I know. I should have been grateful. I had a roof over my head. I was fed three meals a day. I was given an education. In fact, you might say, being at a girls' orphanage doesn't sound all that different from being at a boarding school or one of those fancy so-called finishing schools in Europe. But those schools are for girls who have families—well-to-do families—whereas necessitous girls have no families. Plus, they're poor.

Obviously and blindingly poor. So poor that the people of the good town where the Home was located—the town of Hope (I am not kidding)—looked on us with pity. And condescension. Along with self-righteousness and mistrust. Some of the women called us gypsies when we went into town, especially if one of the little ones acted up. When one of us (who should have known better) swiped some lipstick from the five-and-dime store, we all became little thieves. When one of us (who also should have known better) was caught smoking cigarettes with a local boy behind the old boathouse, we all became tramps. When one of us (expressing what a lot of us felt) refused to sing at the annual church women's Christmas tea, where we were marched in to sing carols as a thank-you for the sturdy beige jumpers the women had sewed for us, every one of them cut from the same pattern, we all became ingrates.

I don't want to give the impression that the entire town of Hope looked down on us, even though it sometimes felt that way. There were decent people, like Mr. Travers, editor and publisher of Hope's one and only newspaper, the *Hope Weekly Crier.* When I finally screwed up my courage just before my sixteenth birthday to apply for a part-time job—he had advertised for a "Goings On" columnist—he gave me a chance. He had me write up a sample column and edit a news story, and then, to my astonishment, he hired me. I felt as if I'd won the Irish Sweepstakes. I was on my way. I had taken the first step toward my dream.

True, it wasn't the most exciting job in journalism. My beat was wedding anniversaries, bridal and baby showers, graduation parties, garden parties, out-of-town visitors and any other social event that the host or hostess wanted everyone in town to know about. I gathered information by telephone, and I didn't have to probe hard to get the facts I needed. All I had to do was talk to the host or, more often, hostess, who would eagerly tell me who had attended the event (we ran as many names as possible), what refreshments had been served, what entertainment had been offered and, in cases where it was deemed important, what the women had been wearing. I didn't use my real name. Instead, at my request, the column ran with the byline Lizzie Cochran. In case you don't know it, Elizabeth Cochrane is the real name of my all-time heroine and role model—Nellie Bly.

(She dropped the *e* from her surname because she thought it looked better that way.)

I know it doesn't sound glamorous. It wasn't investigative reporting, and the events I covered were certainly not earth-shattering. But in a small town like Hope and on a weekly paper like the *Crier*, it was important to cover local happenings. If people wanted to know what was going on in the world, they could get one of the Toronto dailies. But if they wanted to know what was going on down the street, the *Crier* was the paper to reach for.

About the same time I got the job at the *Crier*, I started dating Johnny Danforth. He was a senior at the local high school. He was dreamily handsome, ruggedly athletic and financially well-off. I met him when we literally ran into each other as I was going into the grocery store and he was coming out. It was like something out of one of those romance novels that so many girls bought off the rack by the drugstore checkout. Our eyes met and we knew we were made for each other. At least, that's how I felt. It was also how Johnny said he felt. He didn't seem to care at all when I told him where I lived. Suddenly I was happy. My life had gone from misery to perfection in the blink of an eye. It stayed that way for a couple of months—until one of Johnny's neighbors saw us together and told Johnny's mother.

Mrs. Danforth grilled Johnny, and he, ever the dutiful son, told her everything he knew about me, including my job at the *Crier*. That incensed Mrs. Danforth almost as much as the fact that her son was seeing me, a girl of dubious parentage, on the sly. Then, to make matters worse for me, one of her friends was robbed shortly after the friend had told Lizzie Cochran about the lavish party she was planning for her sister. All the best gifts were stolen. Both Mrs. Danforth and her friend were certain that the robbery was Lizzie's fault. They claimed that I'd tipped off some shady characters, who had then broken into the house and robbed it. They made a big deal out of the fact that I used a pen name. They said I was obviously trying to hide something.

The next thing I knew, Mr. Travers fired me. He said he didn't want to. He said he knew it must seem unfair. (*Seem*?) But advertising revenues had taken a sudden dip, and if that continued, the paper would be in jeopardy. He didn't mention any names. He didn't have to. On top of that, Johnny dumped me. Not right away. Not the minute his mother started in on him. He had to stand his ground long enough to prove that no one told Johnny Danforth what to do. But he did dump me. He sort of tried to be nice about it. "Maybe we should take a break," he said. "I have to concentrate on school." But I knew what was going on. You bet I did. Which is where my story starts, in the summer of 1964.

Chapter Two

MY LIFE GOES UP IN FLAMES

TWELVE HOURS BEFORE the big fire, I was on my way home from the *Crier* office with Mr. Travers's letter in my pocket.

"I'm sorry, Cady," he said when he handed it to me. "I'd keep you if I could, but..."

I was glad he didn't finish his sentence. I didn't want to hear it again. It was like Mrs. Hazelton telling me once that she didn't want to punish me for slapping that townie girl, who, by the way, can best be described as rhyming with *rich*. Did I care whether Mrs. Hazelton wanted to punish me? Of course not. All I cared about was that I was confined to school for a whole month. I also knew that it definitely hurt me more than it hurt her. When Mr. Travers gave me the letter, I thanked him for it and for the opportunity and encouragement he had given me. I hoped he would interpret my gratitude as classy, even though the truth was that it was a calculated move. I wanted him to say good things about me if—no, when—someone called him to ask about my work at the *Crier*. *Never spit into a well you may need to drink from.* I heard a man outside the pool hall say that to his friend one day. I wrote it in my notebook. It made good sense.

I left the newspaper office and had gone barely half a block when Mrs. Danforth emerged from the drugstore. As soon as I saw her, I did an immediate about-face. My plan was to duck through the nearest door. I did not want to face her, not now, not ever again. But the nearest door was the one to the barbershop, where one man was being shaved and two others were chatting while they waited their turn. I couldn't go in there. By the time I decided to walk right past her with my head held high (why shouldn't it be?), Mrs. Danforth had seen me. She didn't speak. I didn't expect her to. Mrs. Danforth saw herself as a superior human being by virtue of her social position. She did not deign to greet or otherwise engage in conversation with anyone whom she deemed beneath her unless she was issuing instructions.

Well, I have eyes the same as she does, except that mine are sharper. I stared right back at her: *Read what you will into that, you miserable cow.* I knew perfectly well that it was Mrs. Danforth who had gone to Mr. Travers, not presuming to tell him his business—*she would* never *do such a thing*—but she felt it was her *duty* to let him know that she and the other ladies of the town, ladies whose husbands were successful businessmen and loyal advertisers in the *Weekly Crier*, were *uncomfortable in the extreme* with my position at the paper and were *ready to complain to their husbands if the situation was allowed to continue*.

The situation. I hated the way that woman talked, always using what Mr. Travers called five-dollar words when a good old everyday five-cent word would do the trick. What Mrs. Danforth meant, plainly put, was that if Mr. Travers didn't get rid of me, Mrs. Travers and her do-nothing lady friends would make good and sure that their husbands canceled their advertising in the *Crier*. In a one-newspaper town, this was blackmail pure and simple, and Mr. Travers caved in even though boycotting the *Crier* would have hurt the businessmen as much as it hurt the *Crier*.

I would have walked right past Mrs. Danforth—I really would have—if Johnny hadn't stumbled out of the store behind her, carrying a large paper bag. He started to say something to his mother but ground to a halt when he saw me. He used to smile at the sight of me. Smile and wrap his arms around me and kiss me on the cheek or the mouth, and then he'd want to go somewhere where we could be alone. This time the little weasel turned red in the face. He looked at his mother with a mixture of shock and apology. *Honest, Mummy, I had no idea we would run into her, I swear! Please don't cancel my allowance*. I couldn't believe I ever loved him, much less dreamed of a future with him. What on earth had I been thinking? Yes, he was cute and smart and loaded with charm, and he had what Mrs. Hazelton would call a *lofty ambition*—he wanted to be a doctor. But when push came to shove, he was a mama's boy. He knew who buttered his bread.

So after taking an initial stand to defend me against his mother's slander, he finally yielded. This happened to coincide with the end of the school year, when he was set to graduate, which was when the car that he'd been promised as a graduation gift suddenly became, in his mother's eyes, a bad idea *because, my dear, I know what those girls are like, they will do anything to land a catch like you, a smart boy, a rich boy, a boy with a future, and, my dear, one of their common tricks—and I do mean common—is to get a boy like you to take them for a drive somewhere, you know what I mean, Johnny, and the next thing you know, she's* enceinte. I'd actually heard her use that word, as if French saved her from having to picture exactly how her son might end up with a pregnant girlfriend.

I stared at Johnny. I knew what he and his mother thought of me, but no one was ever going to be able to say that Cady Andrews was a coward or that she tucked tail and scurried away like a little mouse. I met the same eyes that used to melt me and held them just long enough to let him know that whatever he and his mother thought of me, I thought a thousand times worse of them. They had climbed up on high and judged me, and they had used as their measure not my character but my background, which I had had nothing to do with. Who did they think they were anyway?

Johnny, the coward, blinked first. He averted his eyes and stepped off the sidewalk. Shifting the paper sack to his other arm, he unlocked the trunk of his mother's butter-yellow Buick, the color specially ordered and extra-specially paid for by Mr. Danforth as an anniversary gift. I stepped around Mrs. Danforth and continued on my way. No one spoke a word.

When I got back to the Home, I snuck down to the vast and warrenlike basement and retrieved my suitcase. It was a battered old black thing that I had found under a table at the back of the church-run thrift shop in town and had stashed behind the drying racks where we hung our clothes after fishing them out of the ancient washer. My plan: leave town. I had enough money saved from my wages at the *Crier* for bus fare to Toronto and maybe a couple of weeks at the YWCA. I also had Mr. Travers's letter of reference.

I smuggled my suitcase—already packed—out to the yard and hid it under the shrubs at the back of the property, where no one ever went. I planned to retrieve it before dawn and catch the first bus out of town. By the time they discovered I was missing, I'd be halfway to Toronto, and there wouldn't be anything anyone could do about it. I was almost seventeen. I was legal to quit school. I was legal to get a job. And it was about time I started living the life I wanted instead of the one that had been forced onto me by people I had never met.

So the fire didn't make any difference to me. But I would be lying if I said I didn't care. The Home had been my everything for nearly fifteen years of my life.

I had never experienced a house fire before, and it was a spectacular one. The whole main building where we all slept and ate, the building whose wooden floors, wainscoting, banisters, window frames and trim we washed and polished over and over again until every burnished surface gleamed in the midday sun, all of it was reduced to rubble and ash—and puddles of water, after the fire department arrived, too late to save anything. For hours, it was pure chaos, with girls and staff members running around, counting heads, comforting those who were scared (mostly the Little Ones) and making sure everyone stayed well away from the action. After that, silence. Most of us, I think, were wondering what would happen to us. But not me. I still had my plan, and as soon as things calmed down, I was going to collect my things and go. That was the plan.

Chapter Three

I AM HANDED A MYSTERIOUS ENVELOPE

LEAVING TURNED OUT to be trickier than I had anticipated. The Little Ones were all upset. Most of them cried for at least a while, and all of them had to be soothed and reassured. The seven of us—Toni, Sara, Betty, Tess, Malou, Dot and I—being the oldest, had been cast in the roles of babysitters, older sisters, little mothers and/or amateur nurses. It fell to us to calm and console. The day after the fire we were all summoned by Mrs. Hazelton. Toni talked to her first. Then Betty. Then Dot. Then, just before me, Tess. By the time it was my turn, I had a pretty good idea what was coming.

Mrs. Hazelton, kind and wise (most of the time), launched into the speech that the others had already listened to.

"I know all that," I told Mrs. Hazelton before she got very far. "I know why I'm here."

Mrs. Hazelton sank back in her leather chair and folded her hands carefully on her desk. She was a still person, always. Still, calm and soft-spoken, even though her words were sometimes hard to hear.

"Always the reporter, our Cady," she said. "I suppose you interviewed the others as soon as they stepped out of my study."

You bet I did. And even after I'd learned why Mrs. Hazelton was seeing us each in turn instead of as a group, I told myself that nothing was going to change my plans.

Mrs. Hazelton slid an envelope across the desk to me. "This contains—"

"Some items that my adopted parents handed over when they dumped me here. I know." All of the others had been given something from their pre–Benevolent Home life.

Mrs. Hazelton sat in silence for a moment, studying me with her sharp eyes.

"I'm afraid not, Cady. Not in your case. Your adoption was privately arranged, and since it occurred before you came to us, we were not privy to any documentation. The people who took you in did not provide any information about where you came from originally. The only thing I found was what's in that envelope. It was in the lining of the basket that held the few clothes you came with. And don't you give me that look, Cady Andrews. I am not going to tell you where to find the people who took you in before you came to us. I couldn't even if I wanted to.

Besides, when I sent them a card the first Christmas you were with us, it was returned *Address Unknown*. Unless I miss my guess, the name they gave me wasn't their real name either."

I wasn't surprised. They sounded just like Johnny. They'd traded me in for a newer model like I was last year's Buick. They were cowards too. They didn't want anyone to know they'd taken in an orphan and then changed their minds. So they'd used a fake name. I told myself I didn't care. Why would I? They were nothing to me.

"There is only one item in that envelope, Cady," Mrs. Hazelton continued. "And frankly, I am not sure what to make of it or even if it will do you any good. I—"

"No offense, but I'm not interested." I slid the envelope back to her.

Her back stiffened just a ladylike little.

"Manners, Cady," she warned.

"I said no offense."

"Cady, I know what happened at the newspaper—"

"I don't want to talk about it."

"—but you can't let it make you bitter. People who are bitter are never happy."

"I appreciate everything you've done for me, Mrs. Hazelton, I really do. But what happened at the newspaper helped me make up my mind. Even without the fire, I would be leaving. I was going to have been gone by the time everyone got to breakfast."

"I can't say I'm surprised."

Mrs. Hazelton said things like that all the time, so that if you were small enough and gullible enough, you got the impression that she knew everything there was to know about you, all the time. But she didn't fool me, not anymore. I liked her. I respected her. I think at some point, when I was younger, I even loved her. But that time had passed, and I was aching to start my life, the real one, my life as only I could make it, and never mind anymore what had happened in the past. That was all water under the bridge, so to speak. There was no going back even if I wanted to, which, I guarantee you, I did not.

Mrs. Hazelton laid one hand on the envelope and pushed it across the desk's burnished surface again. "Take it," she said. "In case you change your mind."

I took it, but only to put an end to the conversation. Now I was truly free.

It was midday by the time I'd said my goodbyes and headed into town, where I stood in line at the service counter in the town of Hope's one and only grocery store, behind a plump woman with dimpled elbows and thick ankles that showed no bone. She was holding a pink suitcase in one soft, manicured hand and a matching overnight bag in the other.

She stepped up to the counter, deposited her bags on the floor on either side of her and fussed in her purse for her wallet while she asked for a ticket to Peterborough to visit her sister, who was going in for an operation and needed someone to help her when she got out—not that the clerk seemed remotely interested. She was just a grocery cashier and not much older than me. Her hair, a lacquered beehive, sat as tall as a top hat on her head, and she looked for all the world like a milk cow as she stood at the cash register, chewing a stick of gum with a bored expression on her face.

"Round trip or one way?" she asked when the plump woman paused to take a breath.

"Round trip, of course. I said I was visiting my sister, not moving in with her permanently." The woman shook her head as if this was obvious and the clerk was simple-minded for asking the question. She looked at me for support. *Sorry, lady.* I found myself suddenly fascinated by a display of canned soup at the end of the aisle nearest to me. I'd had it up to here with the women of this town. I was sick of their superior, holier-than-thou attitudes.

The woman paid for her ticket and tottered outside on her fancy high-heeled pumps to claim a seat on the bench in front of the store, where the bus made scheduled stops. I stepped up to the counter and asked for a ticket to Toronto, one way, no explanation. I knew how much the fare was, so I slapped down the exact change. I slipped the ticket into the pocket of my skirt and went outside to wait. I sat as far from the plump woman as possible and avoided eye contact with her. My beat-up little suitcase sat at my feet like an obedient old hound.

I looked down at it and wondered whom it had belonged to and whether that person had ever carried in it every single thing they owned. Was it even possible that such a small suitcase—half again as big as the plump woman's overnight bag—could contain an ordinary person's everything? Or did a person have to be like me, an orphan with practically nothing to call my own and precious few things that were brand-new or bought especially for me? Even my books were secondhand, gleaned, like my suitcase, from the thrift shop. But that didn't matter now. It would never matter again. My old life, the one that would end the moment I set foot on the bus, was a life that had been inflicted on me. My new life was the one I was going to create for myself, one that no one would dictate to me. It was going to be an exciting life, led by a new and improved Cady Andrews—not poor Cady, not unfortunate Cady, not I-wonder-what-will-become-of Cady, but Cady who chose her own path, Cady who made her own decisions, Cady who was the mistress of her own destiny.

I looked down at my suitcase again and made a decision. I swept it up and carried it around to the side of the grocery store, where a row of oversized garbage cans stood ready to receive whatever was thrown their way. There I opened it and started pitching the contents into the first can—two hideous jumpers (handmade by church ladies with a view to longevity, not fashion), one skirt, a size too large, that I'd held together with a safety pin, much to the dismay of Mrs. Hazelton, who'd kept badgering me to put my needle skills to work and *take it in, for heaven's sake*, and one of two floral-patterned blouses. I kept the second blouse, a skirt that I'd finally grown into, a pair of slacks I'd bought for myself, my underwear, hairbrush and toothbrush, and a threadbare hand towel and a bar of soap. And the one book I had taken with me. And the envelope? It was in one of the suitcase's little side pockets, minus the money Mrs. Hazelton had given me. I'd taken that out—money was money, after all—and taped the envelope shut again without looking inside. I had told Mrs. Hazelton I didn't care—and I didn't. I did what I should have done in the first place. I threw it into the garbage can along with everything else. I didn't want to know anything about the past. Why would I? Why should I? I'm not the kind of person who wastes time on things that don't matter, and as sure as the sun comes up every morning, I don't believe in pining for someone—anyone—who shows no interest at all in me. That includes Johnny Danforth and whoever is responsible for my being on this earth in the first place. I snapped the suitcase shut and headed back to the bench. The bus was due any minute.

I was about to sit down again when I saw a man duck down the same alley. He was one of those men you saw around sometimes, even in a quaint, proper little town like Hope. Bums, some people called them. Unfortunates, Mrs. Hazelton said. There-but-for-the-grace-of-God-go-I men. They thrust their hands out for a nickel or a dime when they saw you coming. I heard a sharp clang, and right away I knew exactly what was going on. I jumped up and ran around the side of the store again. Sure enough, the man had lifted the lid from the first garbage can and was rummaging through it, his sun- and wind-burned hands pawing through my clothes, holding up each item in turn and inspecting it before letting it fall back into the trash can. Then he found the envelope. He held it up to the sun, squinting at it to try to see what was inside. He hooked one grubby finger and began to pick at the sealed flap.

"Hey!" I lunged at the man and grabbed one end of the envelope. He hung on tightly. There was no way he was going to let go, not now that someone else wanted it. That only seemed to prove to him that whatever was inside was valuable. "That's mine!" I said.

"It was in the garbage. Finders, keepers." The man's words were slurred and awkwardly formed, and no wonder. He couldn't have had more than a couple of teeth in his mouth.

"It was in the garbage because I dropped it by accident." I tried to jerk the envelope away from him.

"Too bad for you." He gave a mighty yank, and the envelope slipped from my grasp. He grinned at me and hooked his finger again.

There is no reasoning with some people; that's just a fact. And when you can't reason, you have to take action. I stomped as hard as I could on one of the man's too-big, unlaced boots. He howled. I seized the envelope and marched back to the bench. The man started after me but stopped in his tracks when the plump lady fixed her eyes on him. He ducked his head and slunk away. I sat down, envelope in hand.

The woman turned her gaze on me. “You’re one of those girls, aren’t you?” the woman asked.

I hated that question, and I made a resolution there and then to never answer it ever again. People were going to think whatever they wanted to think, no matter what I said. So let them. I took my book out and buried my nose in it until the bus arrived.

Chapter Four

MY DREAMS ARE DASHED

I ARRIVED IN Toronto with no mishaps. I found a room at the YWCA, which was supposed to be one of the safest places for a girl to stay in such a big city. I stowed my suitcase, cleaned myself up and started looking for a job.

I'm not a dreamer like some people, whose names I won't mention. I'm more of a planner. Making a plan and putting it into action works a lot better than mooning around, wishing things were different and longing for the day they will be without actually doing anything to make that happen. I'm practical. I'd already taken steps to put my plan of becoming an ace reporter into action. I'd gotten that job on the *Crier*. I'd amassed a collection of clippings—the "Goings On" column, mostly, but also a few small news items that Mr. Travers had let me cover. I had my letter from Mr. Travers, which described me as reliable, punctual and a good, clear writer. I'd made my way to Toronto. Now all I needed was a job.

I visited every single newspaper in the city—and at every single one, the same thing happened. The receptionist (who was usually a year older than me at the most) directed me to the personnel department, where the personnel manager told me that they weren't hiring typists or secretaries at the moment. When I said I wasn't applying to be a typist or a secretary, I was applying to be a reporter, the personnel manager would tell me, sometimes politely and sometimes not, that they generally didn't hire girl reporters, but if I wanted to, I could leave my name and some clippings and they'd pass it along to the women's-page editors, which I always did because even that would be a foot in the door.

Was I discouraged? Yes, I was. But I had a plan B. You always have to have a plan B.

The next morning I was out again bright and early, knocking on more doors. I had newspaper experience, but it wasn't the only work experience I had. There were plenty of other things I could do—and had done. For example, I would make a crackerjack mother's helper because I had spent years, day in and day out, looking after little ones. I would be a terrific waitress, because I'd carried dozens of trays to girls who were sick in the home's infirmary, and hundreds—no, thousands—from the dining room to the kitchen for washing. Need a maid? I could change beds, do laundry, dust, sweep, mop, vacuum, polish and scrub with the best of them. Advertising for a laundress? I could wash, starch, iron, sew on buttons and mend. Understand, I didn't actually like doing any of these things. But I could do them if I had to.

It took me all of two hours to get a job as a waitress at a restaurant directly across the street from one of the daily newspapers. The best part: newspaper reporters came in all the time, according to Mr. Burt, the manager, who hired me. He didn't seem to care where I came from. All he wanted was someone who was quick and strong and could carry a table-sized tray loaded with daily specials. He said he would give me exactly one shift to prove myself. I danced all the way back to my room and started rehearsing what I would say when I met an honest-to-goodness newspaper editor.

Long story short: I made it through my first shift at the restaurant with nothing more to complain about than sore feet and an aching back. By the end of my first week, I discovered that one of the regulars was the city editor at the newspaper across the street. He came in every day and always ordered the special. One of the waitresses told me he'd been doing that for the better part of eighteen years. He always smiled at me, always asked how my day was going and always left a tip. By the time my second week of work started, after I had practiced in front of the little mirror on the bureau in my room every night, I was ready to make my pitch.

That Monday, I served the city editor the special—corned beef and cabbage with boiled potatoes—took a deep breath, introduced myself and, before he could stop me, gave my speech about why I wanted to be a reporter: it was the only thing I'd ever wanted, I had some clippings to show him and a letter from the newspaper where I used to work, and if he would just give me a chance—

"Hold your horses, missy," he said, glancing up from the clippings that I had produced from my apron pocket. "I'll do better than give you a chance. I'll give you some advice. First of all, these clippings are fluff, not hard news, and I'm a hard-news man. Second, this newspaper"—he squinted at the letter—"the *Weekly Crier*, is that it? That's one of those papers that comes filled with ads for what's on special at the local grocery, am I right? A paper like that, well, I suppose it has its place. But that's not a real paper. Third, and listen closely, young lady, because it's the best advice anyone can give a girl like you, a newspaper office is no place for young girls. Newspaper men—and I count myself among them—are a rough lot. They have to be. They have to pry into people's business and elbow their way into people's houses and offices. They have to do whatever it takes to get the news and get it straight. Believe me, you're better off here. Now, how about fetching me some more coffee?"

I got the coffeepot and brought it over. Why not? It gave me a chance to take another run at him. This time I told him how much I admired Nellie Bly, the famous newspaper reporter, and that it was my ambition to be just like her.

The city editor smiled, which seemed promising, and said, "There's nothing like a freshly brewed cup of java." Then he said, "Kid, I gave it to you straight. This Nellie Bly business, well, I suppose she did a job in her time. But she was the exception, not the rule, and the word among those in the business is that she was more showboat than genuine reporter.

We don't have any room for showboats in my newsroom, even if you had the spunk and the savvy to be like that, which, from what I see, you don't. You look like a good kid. Pretty too. A girl like you will have no trouble finding a husband, and then you can settle down and raise some kids. You don't want to be working with a bunch of roughnecks when you can have your own little family, now do you?"

I was ready to argue—you bet I was. But Mr. Burt, the restaurant manager, sidled up to me and said, "You've got other customers, Cady." He flashed an unctuous smile at the city editor. "I hope you're enjoying your lunch today, Mr. Carter."

"I always do, Burt." Mr. Carter speared a piece of potato and popped it into his mouth.

I went back to work. I carried menus, took orders, hefted trays of food, cleared tables and wiped oilskin tablecloths, and after the lunch rush was over, I stuffed sugar bowls full of paper packets of sugar, refilled ketchup bottles and vinegar dispensers, rolled paper napkins around threesomes of cutlery—knife, fork and spoon—set more slices of pie in the display case to tempt customers and put paper doilies onto saucers ready for glasses of tomato or grapefruit juice. The whole time, I seethed.

Mr. Carter hadn't taken me seriously. Worse, he'd treated me like a silly girl who had no idea how the world worked. But if there was one thing I knew, it was exactly that. Not only did I know how it worked, but I was clear-eyed about it. If I'd started out with any illusions (and I'm sure I did), I'd been stripped of them ages ago. I knew where I stood, or, at least, where I was supposed to stand, and I knew that if I wanted to get ahead, I had to work harder at it than anyone else, because I had no one to rely on but myself. Mr. Carter may have thought he knew me. But he didn't. Not by a long shot.

The next day at noon, I watched for Mr. Carter to come in. He took his usual table and unfolded his newspaper, like he always did, to read while he ate. When I approached his table, he held out his cup without taking his eyes off the story he was reading. He didn't look at me until he realized that his cup had not been magically filled with coffee.

"Oh," he said. "It's you."

"What do I have to do, Mr. Carter?"

"Do? Well, coffee would be a good start."

"To prove myself, I mean. To show you what I can do so that you'll hire me. I'll start anywhere. I'll answer phones. I'll file or type or make coffee. You name it, and I'll do it."

"Now see here, missy, I come in here to relax and enjoy a meal in the middle of what is usually a busy day. I don't come here to be harangued by some starry-eyed little girl like you who read one book too many about some show-offy dame who died before you were ever born."

"All I ever wanted was to be a reporter," I told him. "I'll do whatever it takes. Just tell me what you want."

"I want the special—meatloaf with brown gravy, if I'm not mistaken."

"Give me an assignment. Let me cover something. Let me write something. Anything. You'll see. I'm good."

"Kid, unless you somehow single-handedly stumbled on the story of the century and beat every other reporter on every other newspaper in the city to the punch on it, I don't think there's a thing you can do. I don't hire girls. I certainly don't hire wet-behind-the-ears girls. Now get me my lunch, or I'll have to call the manager."

I got his food. I was tempted to spit on it as I carried it to his table. I slammed it down in front of him. He didn't even look at me. He picked up his knife and fork and set to work, his eyes barely straying from his newspaper.

Was I discouraged yet again? You bet I was. I dragged myself back to my room after work and cleaned up. I was tired. My feet hurt. And so far I wasn't getting any closer to my goal. I reached for my suitcase to get my book. It was pure luck that I had stumbled across it. I'd bought it the previous year. I'd gone into town—actually, I'd snuck into town—and, after making sure that there were no town kids around to make fun of me, slipped into the thrift store run by the church ladies. It was a small place but clean. At the back there were a couple of shelves of donated books that you could buy for a nickel if they were paperback or a dime if they had hard covers. I was always looking for something interesting to read, which excluded the books in the home's so-called library. I wanted adult books. The only adult books on the shelf at the Home were what Mrs. Hazelton called classics—Charles Dickens, Jane Austen, the Brontë sisters and lots and lots of Shakespeare. Poetry too, which I sort of like, depending on what it's about. They were all books that were supposed to be good for us. Uplifting books. You can't believe how many of us had read *Jane Eyre*—and how many of us at one time or another hoped that we would one day meet our very own Mr. Rochester.

Don't get me wrong. I have nothing against Dickens or Shakespeare. But I wanted something different. I wanted the kind of book that the rest of the world was reading, like, say, *Peyton Place*, which turned out not to be nearly as good as I thought it would be, considering that it was strictly off-limits. (I know because Johnny's mother had a copy, and he borrowed it for me without telling her.) To satisfy my craving for reading material, I went to the thrift store once a week, after Mr. Travers paid me, and bought myself one book. That's where I found the one on Nellie Bly—and when I decided what I wanted to do with my life.

Nellie Bly, in case you don't know, was born during the American Civil War. Her real name was Elizabeth Jane Cochrane, and one day she opened the newspaper, just like I did every time I could get my hands on one, and read an editorial that said that girls didn't need an education and they shouldn't aspire to an honest-to-goodness real career because their place was in the home. Their job was to get married, raise children and keep house. You didn't need an education to do that. That got twenty-one-year-old Lizzie's dander up. She wrote a blazing response, which she signed *Little Orphan Girl*. It was so well written and well argued that she was invited to the newspaper office and offered a job.

You have to understand that, at that time, there were very few women newspaper reporters, and they were almost always confined to the women's pages, where they wrote about gardening and fashion and society. But not Nellie. Nellie wrote stories about the poor and the oppressed. She went to Mexico and wrote about the corrupt Mexican government. She got herself committed to a notorious lunatic asylum, as they called them at the time, to write an exposé of how the patients were treated. She wrote about the plight of unwanted babies. She wrote about women who toiled in crowded factories. At a time when women rarely, if ever, traveled the world, she circled it alone in seventy-two days, six hours and eleven minutes.

She was my hero. I wanted to be just like her, only more modern, of course. I wanted to write stories that would turn heads and get people talking. I wanted to step out of my everyday world and into worlds that I'd never visited before, and I wanted to describe them to other people who were as unfamiliar with them as I had been. I wanted to make my living by the pen—or the typewriter. But first I had to find a way in.

When I opened my suitcase to get my book, the brown envelope that Mrs. Hazelton had given me was sitting on top of it. I stared at it. A few days earlier, seven of us, the oldest of the girls at the Home, had been going about our business pretty much as usual. Then our lives had literally gone up in smoke. We Seven, who had spent more time together than a lot of sisters, had dispersed, each with information about our origins, each subsequently stepping out into the world we had largely been protected from, each trying to decide how much and how badly we wanted to know where we had come from and why we had been abandoned.

That's when I got an idea. Nellie Bly got famous by writing about things that no one else had written about. She didn't report on the doings of society matrons. She dug into the lives of working women, poor women who slaved in the sweatshops, earning money by the piece instead of by the hour so that they could keep a roof over their children's heads and put food on their tables. She wrote about women who were locked up in mental institutions. She broke new ground. I decided to do what Nellie had done. That would get Mr. Carter's attention.

I decided to write about us, the seven orphan girls, each on her own adventure. A tingle went through me. It might just work. Most newspaper readers, like most people, were part of a family. Maybe they lived at home with their parents. Maybe they were parents themselves. Maybe their children had grown up and gone off on their own. But as sure as the Rocky Mountains were high, most people were not orphans and knew next to nothing about what it was like to be without parents or a single relative. They might be interested to get the inside story. They might also be interested in following the paths of seven poor orphan girls and their quests for their real identities. But since I had no idea where the other six were at that exact moment, I would start with myself.

It was decided. I had a new plan B.

Chapter Five

I PUT MY NEW PLAN INTO ACTION

I PICKED UP the envelope Mrs. Hazelton had given me—the one I had told her I didn't care about—and ripped it open.

I don't know what I was expecting. Maybe a picture of my mother. Maybe a letter from her, telling me why she'd given me up. But that isn't what I found. The envelope held a single yellowed newspaper clipping. I double-checked, but that's all there was. It wasn't even a whole article. It was just a photograph with a caption underneath. The paper under the caption was ragged, as if someone had torn off the accompanying article—assuming there had been an article.

I looked at the photo. It showed a tombstone in what looked like a small cemetery. The stone in the center of the picture, the one the photographer had focused on, had fallen over. It lay on the ground. Beside it was a piece of stone that had broken off one corner. The photographer had taken the picture so that the engraving on the stone was legible:

Thomas Jefferson
August 10, 1923–June 30, 1948

Mrs. Hazelton had told me the clipping was at the bottom of a basket when I was delivered to the Home. What was it supposed to mean? Did it have something to do with me? Was Thomas Jefferson my father? If so, what had happened to him? How had he died? And at such a young age. He had been just short of his twenty-fifth birthday.

I skipped down to the caption. It started with the name of a town—Orrenstown, Indiana. *Jefferson grave vandalized*, it read. *Sheriff denies Klan involvement*.

Why would anyone vandalize a grave? What had this Thomas Jefferson done? Presumably, someone had thought the Ku Klux Klan was responsible. Why else would the sheriff deny its involvement? But if the Klan hadn't done it, who had? And why?

If I had truly cared about my past, I suppose I would have been disappointed by such meager information. But what a story it made! A vandalized gravestone and rumors of Ku Klux Klan activity was bound to grab people's attention. I could imagine the headline: *Orphan Girl Seeks Parents, Stumbles on KKK Conspiracy*. Or *Orphan Girl Discovers Father Was Grand Dragon of the KKK*. People would definitely want to read about that.

That's how I ended up in the Toronto bus station, buying a ticket to Orrenstown, Indiana. It took a while for the clerk at the ticket counter to find the right bus line and the right connections, because it turned out that Orrenstown wasn't a regular stop. There wasn't even a bench with a sign, like the one in Hope. Orrenstown was just one of the places where a bus going somewhere else would drop you if asked, or where you could flag a bus down if you wanted to go anywhere up or down the line.

One more thing you should know. I stepped off the bus in Orrenstown a couple of days after three students—Michael Schwerner, Andrew Goodman and James E. Chaney—vanished after being released from jail in Neshoba County, Mississippi. Their crime? They'd gone down there to register black voters. The police in Neshoba County claimed the disappearance was a publicity stunt to make Mississippians look bad and insisted that the three had gone back home. A lot of white Mississippians thought that if something unfortunate had actually befallen the trio, well, they'd gotten what they deserved. It never occurred to me that what was happening hundreds of miles away in Mississippi would have any effect on me.

I was wrong.

Orrenstown looked a lot like Hope, except that it was hotter. I took a good look around. To my left were a gas station, a diner, a bank and a hardware store. To my right, a grocery store, a hair salon, a bar, a hotel and a farm-equipment dealership. Other stores and businesses were strung out along the main street, which melted into a two-lane blacktop highway at either end. It was midafternoon, and the sun was high in the sky. I was as stiff as an old lady with arthritis and as thirsty as a suburban lawn in a drought, so I trudged to the diner with its cheery *Come in, we're air-conditioned* sign in the window. The blast of cold air that hit me when I opened the door raised goose bumps on my arms and legs and set me to shivering. It felt delicious. I took a seat at the counter and ordered iced tea. I gulped down half of it as soon as the waitress set the frosted glass in front of me. It was unsweetened, which was a surprise. It was more of a surprise that I liked it that way.

I glanced around. Apart from the waitress and the cook, whom I could see through the service window, there was a grand total of three other people in the diner, all old men, all sitting at the counter, and all wearing straw hats and short-sleeved shirts. All three checked me out. Maybe they didn't get many strangers in town. Or maybe they were dirty old men, the kind Mrs. Hazelton was always warning us about. I paid them no mind. I was too preoccupied with my own thoughts. Was I crazy coming down here and thinking I could discover enough to write a job-winning story? Where would I even start? How hard was it going to be to find out what the picture meant? Did I even want to know? Did I have enough money to cover my expenses here and still get back home? And, most important, was I as intrepid as I hoped I was?

I finished my iced tea and wiped my lips with a paper napkin. The best place to start, I decided, was with the photo. It was all I had to go on. If I found the grave site, I might also find someone who could tell me about the man buried there. My heart raced—I admit it, I was nervous—but I managed to ask the waitress for directions to the local cemetery.

"Which cemetery do you mean?" she asked.

"There's more than one?" That surprised me. From the highway, the town looked tiny. But you know what they say: looks can be deceiving.

The three old men turned to look at me as if their heads were all attached to the same neck.

"There are three," the waitress said. "Oak Grove, Maple Hill and Rolling Meadows."

"Then I guess I need directions to all three."

"You looking for a relation?" one of the old men asked. "Are you one of those folks that's interested in...what do they call it now...generology?"

"Genealogy," the old man beside him said. "It's called genealogy, Earl." He looked around his friend to me. "Is that it? Are you researching your relations?"

"Something like that." Boy, small towns are all alike. Everybody is keen to stick his nose into everyone else's business.

The second old man grabbed a paper napkin from the dispenser on the counter and took a pen out of his breast pocket. He drew a little map.

"Now see here," he said, slipping onto the vacant stool between me and the first old man. "Here's where we are now. You leave here, turn right, then turn left again at the next block and walk, oh, ten minutes, and that'll take you to Oak Grove. From there..."

He walked me through his neat hand-drawn map, giving me directions to all three of the town's final resting places. I thanked him and put some coins on the counter—including a tip for the waitress. I headed for the door, suitcase in hand.

The old man who had drawn the map called after me, "You never did say who you were looking for."

He was right. I never did.

The air above the asphalt rippled like the surface of a lake on a breezy day. The oven-like heat that rose from the pavement engulfed my ankles and calves like thick woollen leggings. I wished I had a hat to protect me from the sun and shield my eyes. A pair of sunglasses would have come in handy too. But I had neither of those things. All I could do was trudge grimly on, following the directions on the napkin and doing my best to ignore the river of sweat that trickled down my back and prickled my underarms.

Once I turned off the main street, I was relieved to discover that Orrenstown's residential avenues were lined with mature trees that formed a protective canopy against the sun's rays. I was able to make faster progress in the cool shade of the elms, maples and oaks that rose from front lawns and dwarfed the two-story brick, stone and clapboard houses. After a few blocks, fenced-in yards gave way to empty lots and meadows. It wasn't long before I spotted a small chapel standing elbow-to-elbow with a low stone wall that enclosed neat rows of gravestones and markers. I had reached my first destination: Oak Grove.

As I got closer, I saw a man in overalls and a short-sleeved plaid shirt, his face ruddy under his straw hat. He was tinkering with the underside of a gas-powered lawn mower that had been flipped upside down on the grass. He glanced up when my shadow fell across him. His knees snapped like kindling when he straightened up. He doffed his straw hat, revealing a forehead as white as milk.

"Can I help you, young lady?"

"I'm looking for a grave."

"Well, I've been tending this place for the better part of half a century. If the grave you're looking for is here, I'll know it." He puffed up, proud of his knowledge.

"This one was vandalized," I told him. "Not recently. A long time ago. Maybe fifteen years."

"Vandalized?" The man scratched his head and plopped his hat back onto his head. "We've never had any vandalism around here. Folks in this town are decent. They bring their kids up right. You must be thinking of some other town."

"Or maybe some other cemetery," I said.

The man was shaking his head before I'd finished speaking. "I don't know what it's like where you come from, but people 'round here don't desecrate graves. Never has happened. Never will happen."

He was wrong, and I had the picture to prove it. I opened my suitcase and pulled out the envelope and the clipping.

The man squinted at the picture and then dug in his pocket for a pair of glasses, which he wore low on his nose. He studied the picture again.

"Oh, *that*." His lips turned down as if he were about to spit out something bitter. "That's different."

"That stone was vandalized," I said. "And the caption says it happened right here in Orrenstown."

"It may say Orrenstown, but it ain't. That cemetery is over in Freemount. Ain't much of anything else there these days. Never really was."

I wondered what he meant.

"Why are you interested in that grave?" he asked. "It can't be because you have any people in there." There was a new look in his eyes now, a harder one, a look of suspicion. "Where are you from? Who are your people? What do you want with a grave in Freemount—'specially that one?"

I didn't care for all the questions. I didn't care for his tone either. He sounded angry, as if I had done something wrong or was about to. He reminded me of Mr. Williams at the five-and-dime back in Hope. He never liked it when I or any of the necessitous girls went into his store. He watched us every second we were there. If we went to the back of the store, he got Mrs. Williams to take over the cash up front while he followed us, keeping a sharp eye on us and being blatant about it. He wanted us to know that he was watching us. He made me so angry that I once stole two cheap rings and some nail polish from his store, just out of spite. I didn't even want them. I threw them in a trash can on my way home.

Instead of answering the man's questions, I said, "Is Freemount far from here?"

"Far enough, I guess." He glared at me. "You one of them college students?"

"What college students?"

"The ones that are heading south, stirring up trouble in other people's backyards when they should be minding what's going on in theirs."

He was talking about the students doing voter registration down in Mississippi.

"No, sir," I said. "If you could point me in the right direction…"

The man stooped to his lawn mower and began tinkering again. "Go back down to the highway and make a right. It's four miles as the crow flies."

I thanked him, flashed a smile—*don't spit in the well*, etcetera—and headed back to the road. When I reached the gate and glanced over my shoulder, the lawn mower was still on its back like an overturned turtle, but the man wasn't bent over it. Instead, he was unlocking the side door to the chapel. I watched him disappear inside.

Chapter Six

I FIND THE MYSTERIOUS GRAVE

THE SUN HAD dipped lower in the sky by the time I got back to the highway, but that didn't offer me any respite because I was walking west, straight into the bright ball of compressed light that hung in front of me like an oversized Christmas ornament, blinding me with its brilliance and blasting me with the heat of an open fire. Sweat poured off me in rivers, drenching my back and pooling in ever-larger circles under my arms until my blouse was soaked through. I would have killed for another glass of iced tea. I would have settled gratefully for a glass of tepid water.

I walked and sweated, and pretty soon I began to wonder if the caretaker at Oak Grove had pointed me in the right direction or told me the truth about how far it was to Freemount. Maybe he'd intentionally steered me wrong. His attitude toward me had certainly grown surly when I told him what I was looking for. But why? What did he know that I didn't know?

I heard a vehicle coming up the road behind me. It was a pickup truck, fire-engine red and spotted with patches of rust. It motored past me before grinding to a stop and slowly backing up. The driver leaned across and shouted through the passenger-side window, "You lost, young lady?"

It was one of the old men from the diner, the one who had drawn the map for me. I approached the truck.

"Not unless I'm going in the wrong direction," I said. "I'm heading to Freemount."

"Freemount?" He looked dumbfounded. "What do you want with Freemount?"

"Does that mean I'm going in the right direction?"

He slid across the truck's bench seat and pushed open the passenger door.

"Hop in. I'll give you a lift."

Mrs. Hazelton would have been horrified if she'd seen me grab the door handle and climb in. Hitchhiking was something boys and men did. It was definitely not something a girl should ever contemplate. Not a decent girl anyway. But the old man was seventy if he was a day. He looked trim, but I was willing to bet I could outrun him if I had to. I could probably wrestle him to the ground too, if it came to that. I was strong. I'd carried countless piled-sky-high baskets of damp laundry out to the clotheslines to pin them up. I'd trucked a little one on my hip for hours at a time. I'd moved furniture and scrubbed floors and dug and weeded gardens. Also, he was wearing Coke-bottle glasses in heavy black frames, which meant that he was probably blind as a newborn kitten without them. In a pinch, I could yank the glasses off his face and throw them into the weeds at the side of the road. I'd be off in a flash while he lurched around, arms out in front of him, like a real-life Mr. Magoo. I slammed the truck door shut, and the old man pressed down on the gas.

"I'm Miles Standish, by the way," he said.

"Cady Andrews."

I left my window cranked all the way down so the breeze would dry my face. For the first time since I'd gotten off the bus, I wondered where I would spend the night. Definitely someplace with a bathtub or a shower. I could hardly wait to scrub off the sweat and grime and climb into my one remaining clean skirt and blouse. Maybe I'd been a little hasty in jettisoning everything else. But at the time I'd done it, I had no idea I was going to make this detour. In fact, just the opposite—I'd been sure that I would end up ripping to shreds whatever was in the envelope.

"What exactly do you know about Freemount, Cady Andrews?" Mr. Standish asked.

"Not much."

He glanced at me.

"Okay, nothing," I admitted.

"But you're interested in the cemetery there?"

"That's right."

"You looking for someone in particular?"

"Thomas Jefferson. But not the president." Although maybe, just maybe, the Thomas Jefferson who was buried in the Freemount cemetery was one of his descendants.

I hadn't thought of that before. Maybe I was related to the third—or was he the fourth?—president of the United States. That would be something. "This Thomas Jefferson died nearly sixteen years ago."

Mr. Standish didn't say anything, not about Thomas Jefferson anyway. "What else do you know about the place?"

"Nothing. Until a half hour ago, I didn't even know it existed. Why?"

"It's a peculiar destination for a young girl such as yourself. There's not much there. Just a few old people too stubborn to move after the flood."

"Flood? What flood?"

"Back in '49. That was the beginning of the end for Freemount, not that anyone around here shed many tears."

What did he mean by that?

Before I could ask, a gas station appeared. Its windows were dark, and the sign over it hung crooked. Mr. Standish slowed his truck to a stop and swept an arm out the open window.

"Here we are."

Beside the gas station, there was a small wood-framed house. Across from it stood what looked like a small bank or post office. A little farther along I saw a closed-down, boarded-up school surrounded by a sagging chicken-wire fence.

"*This* is Freemount?" It looked more like a ghost town.

"I warned you there wasn't much here."

"Not much? It doesn't look like there's anything." Not anything that looked alive anyway. I scanned the desolate landscape. "I don't see a cemetery."

"Ah." Mr. Standish pressed down on the gas again. A moment later I saw a steeple. The truck slowed. I got out in front of a tiny wooden church in the middle of a neatly trimmed lawn edged with well-tended flower beds and shrubs.

"Looks like old Edgar is here." Mr. Standish nodded to a truck that was even older and sorrier-looking than his own. It was parked next to the church and was a depressing industrial gray, like something out of those old black-and-white pictures from the Depression. The front bumper was held on with wire. "He'll see you get safely back to town, if you ask him."

I climbed out of the truck. Mr. Standish tossed me a salute before cranking his steering wheel to turn around. I watched him until he reached the highway and was surprised when he headed back toward town. We hadn't passed any crossroads on our way here, so there was no place for him to turn off before he got to Orrenstown. So where had he been going when he picked me up? And why wasn't he continuing on his way there? That's when it occurred to me: Mr. Standish must have followed me from town. But why? Were people so hard up for gossip around here that they trailed strangers to see what they were up to?

I left my suitcase on the church steps and went around back, where a picket fence that showed more wood than paint corralled a few generations' worth of headstones. An arch with a rainbow-shaped sign attached to it rose above a small gate: *Freemount African Methodist Episcopal Church. Rest in Eternal Peace.*

I dug the newspaper clipping out of my pocket and compared it to the scene in front of me. The fence around the cemetery in the picture looked whiter and straighter than the one in front of me. The headstones were straighter too. But apart from these minor differences, I was sure I was in the right place. I opened the little gate and stepped inside to look for the stone that had been vandalized.

I had no trouble finding it. One corner was still missing, just like in the picture, but the stone was no longer lying on the ground. Someone had righted it. I went closer to read the name and the dates. They were the same. I had found Thomas Jefferson's grave. Now what? What did this man have to do with me?

I heard a whoop. Three small boys with deep-brown skin raced around the side of the church, two of them chasing the third. All three stopped in surprise when they saw me, but I didn't pay them any attention. They were just kids.

Then another boy appeared, this one older and taller.

"I told you all to stay put," he shouted at the youngsters. "You're supposed to be working, and it's church work. Your gran will have a fit if she finds out you didn't do what you was told." He shook his head in disgust. "You know that. You especially, Jacob."

The smallest and skinniest of the boys looked down at his bare and dusty feet, seemingly ashamed of himself—but only for a second. One of the other boys sharp-elbowed him in the ribs and whispered something, and Jacob couldn't seem to stop himself. He burst out laughing.

"Get back to work," the bigger boy snarled, "or I'll tell your granny, and then you'll be sorry."

The three boys skulked back around the church and out of sight. The older boy stayed put. He raised a hand to shield his eyes and frowned at me. I wished he would go back to supervising the little ones, if that's what he was doing, and leave me alone.

He didn't.

He marched over to me and said, "What are you doing?" just as bold as can be, as if I was on his private property instead of in a church cemetery.

"I'm minding my own business," I said. Maybe he would take a hint.

The boy's frown deepened. He leaped over the low fence in one easy fluid movement and wove his way toward me until he could see what I was looking at.

"Why you so interested in that stone?"

That's the main problem with small towns. People have nothing better to do than snoop in other people's business. I wanted to tell him to keep his nose where it belonged. But he clearly knew this church. Maybe he knew more.

"The man who's buried here was awfully young when he died. Do you know what happened to him?" I asked.

"He was shot dead."

I had wondered how the mysterious Thomas Jefferson died. I'd figured illness, maybe. Or some kind of an accident—a car crash or something work-related. But shot? That had never occurred to me.

"Was it a hunting accident or something?" I asked.

"He was shot escaping from prison." The boy all but spit the words at me. What was his problem? Who was he mad at—me or this man who had been dead for over a decade?

"What was he doing in prison?"

The boy glowered at me. "Why do you want to know? What's it to you?"

"I'm just asking."

"He was doing life. For supposedly killing a man."

"Supposedly?"

"It's what I said, isn't it? They said he killed a white man."

A *white* man? I looked up and re-read the sign above the cemetery gate. *African Methodist.*

The boy cocked his head and looked me over, this time with more curiosity than hostility. "You're not from around here, are you?"

I shook my head.

"He was a Negro," the boy said. "They said he killed a white man and they sent him to prison. Then they executed him."

"But you just said—"

"They executed him," the boy said again. "I don't care if you believe it. It's what happened."

Chapter Seven

I VISIT A MORGUE

A CAR HORN tooted. It turned out to be the horn of a cop car. It slid up the dirt road and came to rest in front of the little church. The driver's door swung open and a cop in a tan uniform with a short-sleeved shirt and a cowboy-style hat got out. He had a badge on his left shirt pocket and a pistol holstered to his hip.

"Daniel, how are you?" The cop grinned at the kid.

Daniel did not return the smile. "Good enough, I guess, Sheriff," he said over the sound of boys whooping and shrieking, out of sight but not out of mind—or earshot. "I'd better go. I'm minding some little ones for their gran." He walked away without another word.

The sheriff leaned on the open car door and studied me.

"You must be that girl everyone's talking about, the one with the keen interest in our local cemeteries." There you go. The only way he could have known that was if one of the old men at the diner—or the waitress—had told him.

And since nothing I was doing was even remotely against the law, whoever told him had done so just for the pure joy of passing along a piece of gossip. The sheriff squinted at the stones around me. "Looking for anything in particular?"

I wondered if this sheriff was the same one who had been quoted in the photo caption. Even if he wasn't, for sure he would know the story behind Thomas Jefferson's grave.

"I was looking for this stone." I pointed at it. "That boy was just telling me that the man buried here was shot escaping from prison."

"Well, I guess that's true." He said it casually, as if it were of no importance.

"And that he was sent to prison for murder."

"True again." He removed his hat and ran a handkerchief over his forehead and then around the inside brim. "Your interest is in murderers, is it?"

"I'm just curious about this man. The boy who was just here, he seems to think that he didn't kill anyone."

"Well, I guess you can't blame him," he said. I wondered what he meant by that. "Why is a pretty little thing like you interested in some old murder anyway?"

I didn't want to tell him. If there was a killer somewhere in my family tree, I wanted to know before I announced it to the world. It might color the way people looked at me or influence whether or not they would talk to me, which would make it harder for me to find out what I needed to know. A good reporter has to talk to a lot of people to unearth the truth. And I intended to do just that.

"I'm working on a story."

"A story," he repeated. "Now what kind of story would that be?"

"I'm a reporter," I said. Why not? I was reporting on my search to understand whether the newspaper photograph Mrs. Hazelton had given me would lead me to the circumstances under which I had come into this world. I intended to write up what I was doing and then use it to get Mr. Carter to give me a job. So yes, I was a reporter. I just wasn't being paid to be one.

"You look awfully young," the sheriff said.

"Well, so far I've only written for my school paper," I admitted, if it's possible to admit to a lie. "But I'm going to be a reporter when I graduate."

"Is that so? And you plan to write about this fellow here?" He nodded at the stone.

"I do."

According to the dates engraved on the marker, Thomas Jefferson had died almost a full year after I was born. But he was a black man, which meant there was no way he was my father. I have blond hair, blue eyes and skin that turns red if I get too much sun. The boy, Daniel, had said that Thomas Jefferson had killed a white man. Had his victim been my father? Was that the link between me and Jefferson's grave? Or—and this was also a distinct possibility—was I related to whoever had pushed Jefferson's tombstone over and tried to destroy it? Or had my father been the prison guard who had shot Thomas Jefferson when he tried to escape from prison? I needed to find out.

The sheriff put his hat back onto his head, squinted up at the sun and said, "You planning on staying in town a while?"

"Until I get my story."

"You have kin in these parts?"

"No, sir. I'm on my summer break. I'm on my way home."

"Where are you staying?"

"I'm not sure yet."

"Well then, you'll want to call on Maggie. She takes in boarders. I'm pretty sure she'll have a room for you. Come on, I'll give you a lift back to town." When I hesitated, he said, "I'm Sheriff Hicks. Bradley Hicks. I'm one of the good guys."

The sun had sunk to treetop level, but its descent had done nothing to cool the air. The walk back to town promised to be long and thirsty. I accepted his offer.

Sheriff Hicks circled the front of his squad car and opened the front passenger door for me. Then he climbed in behind the wheel, turned the car around, and we drove back to town.

"So, where's home?" he asked.

I said the first thing that popped into my head.

"New York."

"New York City?" He whistled and shook his head. "I was there once, and I have to tell you, that was more than enough for me. I don't know how folks can live like that, cheek-to-jowl and stacked up so high in the sky you have to rely on an elevator to get you up and down. Not much grass to speak of, either, unless you count Central Park. Me, I like to step out my front door and smell the honeysuckle and the lilacs. I don't even mind mowing the lawn. The smell of fresh-cut grass is worth it. I guess I'm just a country boy at heart."

"Have you lived here long?"

"Only my whole life." He flashed me a smile. "How about you?"

"Me?"

"You lived in New York City your whole life?"

I nodded and hoped he wouldn't ask me too many questions. I'd only seen New York in pictures and movies.

"Where do you go to school?" he asked.

I stared at him, momentarily flustered.

"You said you work on the school paper. College, right?"

I nodded again, pleased that he seemed to have no trouble picturing me as a college student.

"So where do you go to school?"

"Um, California. I...I have relatives in California. I live with them during the school year."

"And you're headed for New York, where you say you're from." He glanced at me again, but he had slipped on mirrored sunglasses, and I couldn't see his eyes. "You wouldn't be telling me a little fib now, would you?"

What? What would make him think I was lying—even though I was?

"I keep my eyes and ears open," he continued. "It's part of my job—making sure my town is safe and free from trouble. And trouble sure seems to be brewing this summer, especially among college students." He stole another glance at me. "You sure you aren't heading up to New York to one of those freedom schools to get your marching orders?"

"No, sir," I said. "I'm going home to see my family."

He nodded and didn't ask any more questions. Instead, he told me about the area, which was mostly agricultural, and about the town, which was mostly quiet.

"They're good, churchgoing people around here. We don't get much trouble. I'd like to keep it that way." He gave me a pointed look.

When we got to town, he turned up a quiet street off the main drag and stopped in front of a large brick-and-clapboard house with a swing on the front porch and a sign on the lawn: *Room and Board. Rooms Available.*

"Maggie will fix you up," Sheriff Hicks said. "You keep your nose clean, you hear?"

I followed the flagstone path up to the porch and rang the doorbell.

No one answered.

I rang again and was about to give up when the inside door opened and a face looked out at me from behind the outer screen door.

"I'd like a room for the night," I said.

The woman, middle-aged, her long hair pinned into a bun, wiped her hands on a cloth and swung the screen door open. "Come on in. You look like you could use a cold drink."

She ushered me through the dark, cool front hall and into a huge, sunny eat-in kitchen at the back of the house with a view overlooking a lawn filled with flower beds and shade trees.

"Have a seat." She busied herself getting down a glass and filling it with icy lemonade from a pitcher in her refrigerator. She set the glass and a plate of lemon loaf in front of me. "Everything is homemade. I'm Maggie. Maggie Nearing."

"Cady Andrews."

Maggie sat in the chair across from mine. "What brings you to Orrenstown?"

"It's a complicated story. Have you lived here long?" If she had, she might be a source for my story—and my quest.

"I was born and raised here."

That was another similarity between Orrenstown and Hope. Most of the people had been born in town and clung to it like burrs to an old sweater.

"But no, I haven't lived here long," Maggie said. "I moved away when I was seventeen. Went to college. Got married. Lost my husband in the war. Did the war-widow thing for a while."

"I'm sorry."

Maggie shrugged. "It was a long time ago, and I was hardly the only war widow. When my dad died two years ago, I moved back here to take over the paper."

"Paper?"

"My dad was editor, publisher, reporter, salesman and circulation manager of the *Ledger*, our local newspaper. He would have added 'chief cook and bottle washer.' Mr. Everything. Of course, the paper was a bigger deal in his day. It ran out of a real office and published six days a week. Covered the whole county. We still cover the county, but there's not enough revenue to publish as often. And I run the paper out of the house. We come out twice a week, and the Wednesday edition is only possible thanks to the weekly sales flyers local merchants use to get people into their stores. Hallelujah for that."

"So you run a newspaper *and* a boardinghouse?"

"Neither of which is making me rich." She laughed. "I have one regular boarder, and from time to time we get salesmen coming through or travelers who need a break from driving. Occasionally, we get a visiting politician. It keeps me going." She nudged the plate of lemon loaf toward me, and I took a piece. It was moist and tangy and reminded me that I hadn't eaten all day.

"I need a room for the night," I said. "And I was hoping you could suggest a place where I can get something to eat. Is the diner any good?"

"It's good enough. But my cooking is better. Let's get you settled, and while you clean up, I'll get supper ready."

I thought about the small cache of paper and coins in my pocketbook. "How much will it be?" I asked tentatively.

"Less than you think. Come on."

She showed me to a large, bright room that overlooked the shady backyard. The big double bed had the thickest mattress I'd ever seen, and when I tried it out, I felt like a princess lying on a bed of feathers.

"The bathroom is at the end of the hall, if you want to take a shower or a bath. There are towels in your wardrobe." Maggie nodded to the large cupboard against one wall. "Supper's in an hour." She left me and went downstairs.

I sat on the edge of the bed, pulled the newspaper clipping from my pocket and smoothed it out so that I could look at it again. Would I get to the bottom of it? If I did, would I like what I found? Would I really want to write it up and show it to a complete stranger? What if I found out something horrible? How intrepid would I feel then?

I set the clipping on the bedside table, took my few clean clothes out of my suitcase and padded down the hall in bare feet to run a bath. I filled the tub fuller than I had ever been allowed to at the Home. There was a bottle of bubble bath sitting at the end of the tub. I twisted off the cap and smelled the contents. Lilac. I glanced around nervously, even though there was no one to see me, and tipped just the smallest amount of the violet liquid into the bath. The water started to foam. I stripped down and slipped into the hot water, stretching out full length and resting my head against the back of the tub. Slowly, I started to relax. It wasn't until I heard Maggie's voice calling my name from outside the door that I realized I'd fallen asleep.

"Five-minute warning," Maggie called through the door.

"Coming," I called back.

I leaped up, pulled the plug and toweled myself dry. It didn't take long. Before I went downstairs, I cleaned the tub—a habit that had been hammered into all of us at the Home—and hung my towel to dry. I took the newspaper clipping downstairs with me and followed the aroma of cooking into the kitchen, where the table, covered in an oilskin cloth, had been set for three. A man was already seated in one of the chairs. He was middle-aged, like Maggie, and was wearing overalls and a short-sleeved shirt like the old men in the diner. His face and his arms were brown from the sun, but his forehead was a band of blinding white.

"This is Arthur Malone," Maggie said. "Arthur, this is Cady. She's staying the night. Arthur comes through here every year about this time and stays until after harvest. There's always someone around here who needs a field hand, isn't that right, Arthur?"

Arthur nodded.

I slipped into one of the two vacant chairs.

"What do you do the rest of the year?" I asked him.

Maggie answered for him. "He's got a place in Florida, in the Keys. He says all he does down there is kick back and fish."

"Marlin," Arthur said. "And tuna. I've been trying to get Maggie to come down for a visit, but so far she's turned me down every time."

"I have a business to run." Maggie set down a platter of fried chicken, a bowl of potato salad and another of peas. Moisture had beaded up on the glass pitcher of iced tea in the middle of the table.

"Business can wait," Arthur said firmly. There was a real fondness in his eyes when he looked at Maggie. "Everyone has to take a vacation from time to time."

"If they can afford to, which I can't." Maggie sat down and poured the iced tea.

The food was passed around, and we all served ourselves. I was nervous at first. The only person I had had a meal with outside the Home was Johnny, and that was just hamburgers at a place on the edge of Hope where none of his mother's friends were likely to see us. I ate slowly at first, the way Mrs. Hazelton had said young ladies should eat. But the chicken was the best I'd ever tasted, crunchy on the outside and moist on the inside. The potato salad had chunks of onion and celery in it and pieces of hard-boiled egg. And the peas were sweet and fresh. Before I knew it, I had cleaned my plate. I looked up to see both Maggie and Arthur grinning at me.

"Well, someone sure is hungry," Arthur said.

My cheeks stung. I knew I must be as red as the boiled beets that had appeared on the table at the Home every Sunday night.

Maggie offered me more chicken, but I was too embarrassed to accept.

"Go ahead," Maggie urged gently. "There's nothing that makes a cook happier than an appreciative eater."

"There's nothing that makes a boarder happier than a landlady who cooks like Maggie," Arthur said, serving himself some more potato salad.

I looked at the golden-brown chicken. It had sure tasted good. One more piece wouldn't hurt. It wasn't as though anyone else was going to go hungry. I chose a drumstick and accepted the bowl of potato salad from Arthur. I added a spoonful of peas to my plate and ate until I was stuffed, something I'd rarely had the chance to do. When Maggie got up to clear the table, I jumped to my feet.

"Let me do that." I scraped the plates and set them into the sink.

"There's a pie on the counter," Maggie said. "And some dessert plates to serve it on."

The pie was apple sprinkled with cinnamon, and it was warm from the oven. The flaky crust melted in my mouth. This time when Maggie offered seconds, I didn't hesitate. I said yes right away. I'd never tasted anything so divine. By the time I had cleaned my plate and leaned back in my chair, belly pleasantly distended, I felt relaxed. Maggie poured mugs of coffee for everyone. When she was seated again and stirring a teaspoon of sugar into her coffee, I pulled out the newspaper clipping and handed it to her. She examined it closely.

"I'm pretty sure that came from the *Ledger*," she said.

"Do you know anything about what happened?" I asked.

She shook her head and passed the clipping to Arthur.

"I heard about this," he said. "It was before my time, but when I first started coming through here six or seven years ago, looking for work, someone made mention of a murder in town."

"Murder?" Maggie snatched the clipping from Arthur and looked at it again. "It doesn't say anything here about a murder."

"Doesn't say it, but that's what happened." Arthur sipped his coffee, which was a light tan color from all the cream he poured into it. "That fella Jefferson murdered some white man that was passing through town. At least, that's the way I heard it. Jefferson got life. He was shot trying to escape from prison."

"Well, that's news to me," Maggie said. "Right after I came back here, I went straight to the morgue to read up on what had gone on in my absence. But I didn't see anything about a murder. Or about anyone named Thomas Jefferson."

"I'd love to take a look at the morgue myself," I said. Every newspaper had a morgue. It was where back issues were kept. "If you'd let me, that is."

"Be my guest." Maggie stood up and led me to a room beside the kitchen, which I could see was the newspaper office. It was equipped with a couple of desks, two typewriters, a phone and some filing cabinets. Maggie pointed to a door beside one of the desks. "It's in the cellar. The light is at the top of the stairs. I have to warn you though—one of the shelves collapsed a while ago, so things aren't in strict chronological order."

I made my way down a flight of wooden stairs into a room lined with shelves. On one side of the room, they were new and sturdy. On the other side, they were older, water-stained and sagging. Besides the shelves, there were half a dozen six-drawer filing cabinets. If the photo I had been given came from Maggie's newspaper, then I would find it down here, together with any news story that might have accompanied it. I would finally find out exactly what had happened and maybe get some clue about what Thomas Jefferson and his grave meant to me.

Chapter Eight

I DISCOVER THAT NOTHING IS AS EASY AS IT LOOKS

THE NEWSPAPERS, IT turned out, weren't bound into neat volumes the way they were back at the *Weekly Crier*. And Maggie was right about them not being in strict chronological order. In fact, they were in no order whatsoever that I could discern. From the look of things, whoever had cleaned up after the old shelf collapsed had simply scooped up stacks of newspapers and piled them willy-nilly on the new shelf.

I had no idea when the murder had been committed or how long Mr. Jefferson had been in prison before he'd tried to escape, so I worked my way through the stacks, pulling out all of the issues from the time of his death back to the beginning of the 1940s. I separated the papers into eight piles, one for each year. That alone took me more than an hour. Once I'd done that, I thumbed through the papers in reverse order, beginning with June 30, 1948, the date on Mr. Jefferson's gravestone. I didn't have to go far—only three days—before I spotted a brief news item: *Thomas Jefferson, 25, of Freemount, was fatally shot while escaping from prison. 'It was a daring attempt,' Warden Albert Drudge said. 'I hate to think what he would have done had he made it.' Jefferson was serving a life sentence after being convicted of the first murder in this county in more than two decades.*

That was it. No larger or related articles, no pictures, not even the date the murder had occurred. I flipped through the rest of 1948 in case it had been an open-and-shut case—maybe Mr. Jefferson had pled guilty—followed by a quick stop in prison before the attempted escape.

There was nothing. But that didn't mean I was ready to quit. If Jefferson had committed the county's first murder in decades, the *Ledger* must have covered it. I paged through the papers from 1947. Then 1946. Still nothing. Nothing in 1945 or 1944 either. I even went through 1943, just to be sure.

I drew a complete blank.

I looked in exasperation at the piles of *Ledgers*. It didn't seem possible that the local newspaper had neglected such a big event. There must be something. That's when I noticed that the stack of papers for 1947 was half the size of the ones for other years. It turned out there were more issues missing than were in the pile. Once I put them in chronological order, I realized that every paper from mid-April until the end of October was missing. Was that it? Was the reason I'd found no mention of the murder or the trial that they had happened after mid-April and before November?

In other words, during the time covered by the missing papers.

But why were they missing? Had the murder been such hot news that those issues had sold out? I supposed it was possible. Or maybe someone had gotten rid of them on purpose. But why?

I set all of the newspapers back on the shelf. The *Ledger* must have covered the murder and the trial. There had to be something somewhere. I looked at the bank of filing cabinets. I opened the top drawer of the closest cabinet and shuffled through the folders inside. They were all old. Some of them went back to the 1920s. The newest ones—at least, in this drawer—were from the late 1950s.

I stepped back, located the drawer marked *J* and worked my way from *JA* to *JE* and then from there to *JEF*. There were two files with the name Jefferson on them, but neither with the name or even initial *T*. I pulled out the folder for M. Jefferson. The papers inside were all from 1951 and were about May Jefferson, who ran successfully for the school board. W. Jefferson was a politician in the state capital who ran afoul of the locals by lobbying against the placement of the new state-funded mental hospital in the county. That was it for Jeffersons. I know because I combed through the whole drawer and even checked the *Is* and the *Ks* (there weren't many), in case information related to the murder had been misfiled. I wished I'd thought to ask the name of Thomas Jefferson's victim. It was possible information had been filed under his name.

I trudged upstairs empty-handed. Maggie and Arthur were still at the kitchen table, but it had been cleared and a checkers board now sat between them. Maggie made a move before glancing up at me.

"Did you find what you were looking for?"

"No." I was discouraged. "Did anything unusual happen in town between April and October in 1947?"

Maggie looked puzzled. "I was long gone by that time. What did you have in mind?"

"I know there was a flood in 1949. Was there one in 1947?"

"If there had been, I would know about it. Dad would have told me. No, 1949 was the first flood in decades, and there hasn't been another one since."

"What about a fire?"

"I suppose it's possible." She looked at Arthur. He shook his head.

"I mean a fire in the newspaper office—or in this house."

Maggie shook her head. "Why are you asking?"

"Because every newspaper between April and October 1947 is missing."

"That's odd. Did you check the files? Maybe..."

"There's nothing there either." I thought for a moment. "Is there any other way a person could find out about a trial that took place in this town besides reading about it in the newspaper?"

"The courthouse must have records," Maggie said. "And transcripts. If it's important to you, you could go over there tomorrow." She looked me over. "*Is* it important?"

I nodded, but I didn't want to talk about it. Not yet anyway. Besides, it was getting late.

I was at the courthouse when it opened at nine in the morning. A man who looked like a security guard unlocked the front door, and I followed him into a two-story atrium floored with marble and hung with paintings of former mayors, all men. When I asked about trial transcripts, he directed me to the basement.

"Take the stairs next to the elevators." He pointed.

The basement was brighter than I'd expected, thanks to the neon lights that ran like landing-strip markers down the center of the ceiling. The hallway formed a large square. I know because I'd made a circuit of it and was almost back where I had started before I saw a sign that read *Court Archives*. I knocked. A muffled voice called from inside: "Enter."

A thin man with skin so pale he looked as though he'd been held prisoner in this basement for decades looked up from his folding chair at a small table behind a broad counter. He was stirring cream and sugar into coffee poured from a thermos. He stared at me and waited for me to speak.

"Is this where trial transcripts are kept?" I asked.

The man stirred his coffee, took a tentative sip and nodded with satisfaction. He didn't speak. Maybe he couldn't. Or maybe he was hard of hearing.

I raised my voice. "I'm looking for the transcript of a trial that I think happened about fifteen years ago."

The pale man took another sip of coffee and dabbed his lips with a cloth napkin.

"Name of the accused?"

"Jefferson. Thomas Jefferson."

"And your interest?"

"I beg your pardon?"

"What is your interest in the trial transcript? This isn't the public library. We're not here for your entertainment. This is the justice system."

Did that mean he wouldn't help me unless I had a valid reason for wanting to see the transcript? Should I tell him what I had told the sheriff, that I was researching a story? Or...

"Miss Nearing sent me," I said. Technically, that was true. "From the *Ledger.*"

The man rolled his eyes. "That woman is always poking around where she doesn't belong." He stood up, and I was surprised to find that he was considerably taller than me. "She makes more hay out of a 'no comment' than anyone else I know. Jefferson, you say?"

"Yes."

He got up and began a slow trek between the floor-to-ceiling shelves that filled the room behind the counter. Each shelf held cardboard file boxes stacked two high and six across. I strained over the counter to follow his progress, but he soon disappeared from sight. I waited.

At long last he returned with a dust-coated box, which he dropped on the counter. It landed lightly, which wasn't encouraging. A murder trial was a serious and complex thing. The box should be full of pages and pages of transcripts and other documents. It should land with a satisfying thump.

The man removed the lid, and I leaned forward to look inside. With a cluck of annoyance, he tilted the box away from me, blocking my view. He pulled out a folder and opened it to reveal a single sheet of paper. He read it and looked into the box again.

"No transcript," he announced.

"But there must be one. This is where they're kept, isn't it?"

"No. Transcript." He spoke the words slowly and loudly, and with unconcealed impatience.

"Is there someplace else it could be?"

"Someone must have borrowed it and not returned it. That happens sometimes. They all know they're supposed to return what they borrow, but some of them don't."

I thought of the public library back home. When you borrowed a book, a librarian stamped the card in the back so that you knew when to return it. She also removed a small slip from the pocket glued inside the cover. This had the name of the book on it, and she wrote in a neat hand the name and library card number of the borrower.

"You must have a record of who has it," I said.

The man gave me a withering look. "If I did, it would be in the box. But it isn't. There's just the court assignment."

I had no idea what that was, but it might contain something helpful.

"May I see it?" I asked.

He grudgingly obliged. The assignment sheet told me nothing except the name of the accused, which I already knew, and the number of the courtroom—2—where the trial was held. It was dated July 16, 1947.

"There's nothing else?"

He tipped the box so that I could see for myself that it was empty.

"Do you know where else I could find information about the trial?"

"I'm in charge of records. I'm not a public-information officer." He dropped the file back into the box, replaced the lid and sat down to his coffee. The curl of his lip after he took a sip confirmed what I suspected, that it had grown hopelessly cold. I left him to his grumbling.

Something was definitely wrong. All the newspapers for months before and during the trial were missing. There were no files anywhere in the newspaper morgue that made any reference to Thomas Jefferson, even though he had been convicted of one of the town's rare murders. And now the trial transcript and documents were missing. Was it all a coincidence or was something else going on?

Chapter Nine

I START ASKING QUESTIONS

IT WAS JUST after ten o'clock in the morning by the time I left the courthouse, but already it was as hot as the inside of an oven. The sky was a clear, deep blue, with not a cloud anywhere and no hint of a breeze. It was going to be one of those days when the sun could bake a person as crisp as a Christmas turkey.

Now what? Where should I go from here?

Women in summer dresses and hats, shopping bags over their arms, glided from store to store on the other side of the street. Little children frolicked in a small park, playing while their mothers or babysitters sat on benches in the shade. A postman trudged slowly down the sidewalk, dropping mail through slots and into boxes. Two pickup trucks sat in front of the hardware store while men in short-sleeved shirts and overalls chatted with each other. A kid pushed open the door to the diner.

That gave me an idea. It was early, but old men are like old women: they have nothing better to do than sit around and shoot the breeze. The only difference is that they don't do it over tea at each other's houses. Instead, they drive their wives to town to shop and do their errands while they sit and wait for them over a cup of coffee somewhere. I crossed the street.

Sure enough, three old men sat over mugs of coffee at a table near the counter. One of them was Mr. Standish. He glanced up when I came in—so did his companions—so I smiled and waved.

"Well, if it isn't Cady Andrews." Mr. Standish smiled as if he was glad to see me. "How did you make out yesterday?"

I approached the table and nodded pleasantly at all three men. "I was hoping I would run into you again."

Mr. Standish beamed at me. "Is that so?"

"Actually, I'm hoping you can help me. I've been trying to find out about something that happened here back in the 1940s."

The three men exchanged glances.

"Well, we were all here then," Mr. Standish said. "Why don't you sit down and tell us what you're after, and we'll see what we can do?" He got to his feet, clutching the back of his chair until he could straighten up. "Damned arthritis," he muttered. He pulled out an empty chair for me, and I sat down. "This here is Lloyd Selig," he said, nodding to the man on his left, a ruddy-faced, blue-eyed man with a paunch like Santa Claus's. "And this is Marcus Drew." Mr. Drew was one of those naturally thin men who are all skin and bone. His ears stuck out from the side of his head like the handles on a sugar bowl.

I shook hands all around while Mr. Standish beckoned to the waitress for another cup of coffee.

"Now, what do you need to know, young lady?" he asked.

"It's about a murder."

Mr. Selig and Mr. Drew frowned. Mr. Standish looked intrigued.

"This is about that fellow Jefferson whose grave you were looking for yesterday, isn't it?" he asked.

I nodded. "Were you here when it happened, when Mr. Jefferson went on trial for murder?"

"Yup. We all were," Mr. Standish said.

I felt a surge of excitement. Finally I had found someone who could tell me what had happened.

"What do you want to know about that for?" Mr. Selig asked. He was peering at me the way Miss Webster at the Home had inspected the little black pellets in the pantry the time we had a mouse infestation.

"I want to write about it."

"You're a reporter?" Mr. Drew's eyes narrowed, and he regarded me with suspicion.

"Sort of. I work on the newspaper at school."

"Oh. College student, are you?" The curl of Mr. Selig's lip led me to believe that he did not hold college students in any higher regard than he did reporters. "Not one of those troublemakers we keep hearing about, I hope. Kids that have nothing better to do than make a mess in other people's backyards."

"No, sir. But I am interested in law, and I heard about this case."

"Is that so? What did you hear?" Mr. Selig was definitely the least friendly of the group. Every word he spoke was heavily tinged with mistrust.

"Now, Lloyd, take it easy on the girl," Mr. Standish said. "She's young, and she's not from around here."

"Exactly," Mr. Selig said. "All the more reason for her to keep her nose out of where it doesn't belong."

"There's not much to tell," Mr. Standish said, ignoring Mr. Selig. "Jefferson grew up around here—over in Freemount. There used to be a lot of little towns like that around here, settlements of runaway slaves who put down roots, or tried to, in these parts before the war." It took me a few seconds to understand that he meant the Civil War. "More of them came up here after it was over. Tried to make a go of farming. The land is generally pretty good around here. But the plots were small, and after a while a lot of people moved on, especially when the war—the one against Hirohito and Hitler—came along. There were lots of jobs to be had making munitions, tanks, airplanes, you name it, and a lot of the colored folk left here to try their luck. Pretty soon the only people left were the old folks. They hung on as long as they could. Jefferson's mother was one of them. She made up her mind to stay put until her son came back."

"He went to work in a factory?" I asked.

"Nope. Signed up to fight the Germans. Joined the 761st Tank Battalion. They called themselves the Black Panthers because they'd be taking on the German panzer tanks. They were all colored fellas. The 761st saw action at Omaha Beach and the Battle of the Bulge. As I understand it, young Jefferson came home with a reputation as a war hero."

"Or so he said," Mr. Selig muttered.

"Also came back with a chip on his shoulder," Mr. Drew said, clearly unimpressed. "Strutted around town in his uniform as bold as you please. Wouldn't stand aside for a woman coming down the sidewalk. Acted like he thought the whole world should have changed just because he fought over there. Acted like he was the only one who'd gone off to war, even though plenty of us had sons who enlisted."

"Young Jefferson had some strong opinions, that's for sure," Mr. Standish said. "He'd tell anyone who would listen—"

"And even those that wouldn't," Mr. Selig chimed in.

"—that any man who was good enough to risk his life for his country should be the equal of any other man, regardless of the color of his skin." He smiled softly at Cady. "You're young, and you're not from around here, so maybe you won't understand. But people in Orrenstown and in other towns in these parts had been doing things a certain way for generations. Change comes hard. The way Jefferson talked and behaved, well, it rubbed people the wrong way."

"Is that what led to the murder? Did he get into a fight with someone?" I asked.

"In a manner of speaking."

"He murdered his buddy, that fella he brought back with him," Mr. Drew said.

"He and Jefferson met overseas, and to hear Jefferson tell it, he saved this fella's life and they became fast friends," Mr. Standish said.

"Those Frenchies opened their arms to colored entertainers," Mr. Selig said disapprovingly. "Treated them all like something special."

"He was French?" I asked.

"As French as the Eiffel Tower. Spoke with an accent."

"And he sure did seem to like the Jefferson boy," Mr. Drew said. "He stayed with Jefferson's family over there in Freemount." He shook his head, as if all these years later he still couldn't believe it. "The two of them swanned around together. I heard they were thinking of starting some kind of business."

"A garage," Mr. Standish said. "Apparently, that fella—LaSalle was his name—was a good mechanic. Jefferson, he wanted to invest in a gas station on the highway. They were thinking his mother could run a little diner on the side, and LaSalle would take care of the car repairs."

"Did someone object to the plan?" I said.

"Well now, I can't say that everyone thought it was a crackerjack idea." Mr. Drew drained his coffee and raised his cup to signal for a refill. "But I guess you could say that no one had much of a chance to do much objecting, because the next thing anyone knew, Jefferson killed LaSalle and hid the body to make it look like LaSalle lit out for home."

"But you said they were friends. Why would Mr. Jefferson kill his friend?"

"*Mister.*" Mr. Selig shook his head in disgust.

Mr. Standish glanced at Mr. Drew, who was focused on the tabletop.

"Go ahead and tell her, Marcus," Mr. Standish said. "It was a long time ago. It's all water under the bridge now."

Mr. Drew was silent for a moment. When he finally looked up, his eyes were hard. "I guess you could say I got into an argument with Jefferson. I was sick and tired of the way he was acting, like he was more important than anyone else. Like we owed him something. My boy John served over in Europe. Died there too, after winning himself a Purple Heart for saving six of his comrades. But I tell you what, if he'd come back with all the medals he earned pinned to his chest, he would never have strutted around like the cock of the walk. He was a good boy. Modest. So when Jefferson near ran me off the road one day, well, I stopped and called him out. I told him exactly what I thought of him and all his strutting. I put him in his place."

I wondered what he meant but was afraid to ask. Mr. Drew was caught up in his memories, and they had obviously opened a hurt deep inside him.

"That LaSalle fellow, he was there too. But he didn't say much. Guess he didn't think it was any of his business. When they were finally leaving, I heard Jefferson tear a strip off LaSalle for not standing up for him. Next thing anyone knew, LaSalle was found floating in the river with his head bashed in."

I looked at all three men in turn as I thought about this new information—not just the words these men had spoken but also the tautness or lack of it in their lips and the fire or ice in their eyes. I wondered where Mr. Drew kept his son's Purple Heart. I also wondered if he ever wished his son had saved himself instead of those six other soldiers, other men's sons.

"From what you told me, it sounds like a lot of people might have had something against Mr. Jefferson."

"What's that supposed to mean?" Mr. Selig demanded. "Are you saying you think someone else killed that fella, not Jefferson?"

"I've met at least one person who seems to think he didn't do it," I said.

All three men shook their heads, and all three opened their mouths to speak. But Mr. Standish and Mr. Drew deferred to Mr. Selig.

"He confessed." Mr. Selig crowed the words as if he'd just won the biggest Bingo prize of the night.

"He did?" Then why had the boy at the cemetery given me the distinct impression that he believed Jefferson was innocent?

"He did indeed." Mr. Selig leaned back and crossed his arms over his chest. He reminded me of Mr. Entwhistle, the inspector who had come to the Home twice a year to make sure everything was running according to regulations. He always stayed for dinner, and he loved nothing better than to lean back in his chair while his meal digested in his ample belly and tell all of us senior girls that we had better apply ourselves to household skills because, should we ever be so lucky as to attract a husband, he would be expecting someone who could keep a clean house and set a plentiful table. He'd made my stomach turn. If there was a Mrs. Entwhistle, I felt sorry for her.

Mr. Standish gave me a sympathetic smile. The other two glowered at me as if I'd gotten exactly what I deserved.

"The Jefferson boy got life for what he did. I guess he couldn't take it," Mr. Standish said. "He tried to escape. He got shot. That was the end of it."

"What about Mr. LaSalle?" I asked. "Where is he buried?"

Mr. Standish looked at his two friends, not at me, when he answered. "I believe they shipped him back home."

Chapter Ten

I HEAR THE OTHER SIDE OF THE STORY

I DON'T REMEMBER making a conscious decision to return to Freemount. All I remember is leaving the diner and walking in the general direction of Maggie's, and somewhere along the way I decided to keep walking so that I could think. There's something about walking, especially alone, that relaxes me and switches on my thinking brain. Maybe it's the rhythm of my feet or the roll of my gait. I'm not sure. All I know is that when I have a problem, I often find myself taking a long walk. Sometimes I hit on the solution to my problem. Sometimes I don't. Sometimes all that happens is that I learn to relax about whatever it is. Either way, a walk always makes me feel better.

So I walked. And walked. I walked until I saw the sagging buildings of Freemount up ahead, and then I picked up my pace, because suddenly I was impatient to get there. When I finally reached the abandoned hardware store, I stopped and looked around. Besides the church in the distance, there was a wood-framed building with a faded General Store sign on the false facade over the door. I went closer. The windows were streaked with dust, and a chain and padlock secured the door. There was a café next door, also empty but with checkered cloths and little flower vases still on the tables. The flowers in the vases were all brown and dried. A dead fly lay on one of the tables near the window, its legs in the air. Next to the café was a hair salon, also deserted, and down the street was an abandoned garage with signs advertising brakes, shocks, oil changes and bodywork. Where the gas pumps once sat were patches of weeds. Was this the garage that Mr. Jefferson had hoped to buy? Up the street behind the garage was a house. White sheets and pillowcases hung from a clothesline in the side yard. Someone still lived there. Mr. Standish had said that it was mostly old people who had hung on in Freemount. I wondered what kind of story one of them might tell.

The house was as old as the rest of the buildings in town. Once upon a time its wood siding had been painted yellow. Now the paint was badly sun-faded, washed out to the color of butter. The lower part of the house, right up to the small picture window, was gray, the wood warped and swollen. I was willing to bet it was a result of the flood.

I started down an uneven path to the front porch. A boy came around the side of the house, a watering can weighing down the left side of his body. He didn't look up. He set the watering can down in front of a flower bed that ran nearly the whole length of the porch. He knelt beside it and began to pull weeds. He was the boy from the cemetery. Daniel.

I hesitated. He hadn't been friendly when I met him, but he obviously lived here. Maybe he could tell me where to find Thomas Jefferson's mother.

"Excuse me," I said.

Daniel craned his neck to look at me.

"What are you doing here?"

Still not friendly.

"I'm looking for someone."

He stood up and looked me over. "Where are you from anyway?"

"No place you ever heard of." I would have staked my life on it.

"Try me."

I did. I was right. He'd never heard of Hope.

"Where's that?" he asked.

Before I could answer, the front door opened and a woman came out, her dark skin looking even darker against her bright-yellow dress and the crisp white apron over it. Her mouth was open, as if she had been about to say something until she noticed a stranger in her yard. She looked inquiringly at Daniel. He shrugged.

"Well, good morning," the woman said in a lilting voice, like a song. When she stepped out of the shade of the porch, I saw gray hairs peeking out from under the colorful cloth wrapped around her head. "Daniel, where are your manners? Aren't you going to introduce me?"

"This is the girl I told you about, the one who was asking all those questions about TJ."

The woman peered at me again but didn't say anything.

"She says she's looking for someone," Daniel said.

The woman looked surprised. "You know folks here in Freemount?"

"Not exactly. But I was hoping to find a Mrs. Jefferson."

"I'm Mrs. Jefferson. Lila Jefferson."

"Thomas Jefferson's mother?"

She nodded. Tiny lines appeared over the bridge of her nose.

"Why are you looking for me?" she asked. "You aren't one of those students I've been hearing about on the news, are you, come to stir things up?"

"No, ma'am. But I was hoping to talk to you about Mr. Jefferson."

"Mr. Jefferson? My husband?"

"About Thomas."

"What about him?" Daniel demanded. He'd abandoned his weeding and gone to stand beside Mrs. Jefferson.

"There's no call for that tone of voice, Daniel," Mrs. Jefferson said. She smoothed her apron. "What's your name, honey?"

I told her.

"Well, Cady Andrews, come in and have some lemonade."

The house was modestly furnished. Nothing was new, but everything was well kept. The dining-room table gleamed, little lace doilies sat on the arms of the sofa and matching armchairs—both a faded floral pattern—and the wood floor, although not shiny, was dirt- and dust-free. I followed Mrs. Jefferson through to the kitchen at the back of the house. Its three spotless windows were open, but the kitchen was hot despite the gentle breeze from outside. Mrs. Jefferson waved me into a chair, pulled a pitcher of lemonade out of an old refrigerator and poured me some. I had to hold myself back from gulping the whole glassful right down.

Mrs. Jefferson sat at the table with me.

"Now," she said, "what do you want to know?"

"And why?" The second voice came from the kitchen doorway. It was Daniel. He eyed me with suspicion. "Why are you so interested in TJ?"

"You be polite, Daniel Jefferson," Mrs. Jefferson said. So Daniel was a Jefferson too. Maybe a grandson. Mrs. Jefferson turned back to me. "Never mind Daniel. He takes after all the men in this family—headstrong and impatient. I've been trying to teach him some manners, but so far it hasn't taken." She looked pointedly at the boy, who regarded her with a cool expression, his arms crossed over his chest.

"You don't even know who she is," he protested. "She has no business prying into our family."

Mrs. Jefferson ignored him.

"Now then, honey. You were saying?"

"I was hoping you could tell me about Mr. Jefferson and what happened when he came back from the war."

"Why?" Daniel glowered at me. "Why do you want to know that?"

Mrs. Jefferson got to her feet. Her hands rested on her ample hips, and she glowered at the boy. “You have two choices, Daniel. You can either listen quietly to what this young lady has to say, or you can get back to your chores. If you stay, I don’t want to hear another word from you. Do you understand me?”

Daniel turned angry eyes on her. She glared back at him. He bowed his head slightly, just enough to signal defeat.

“Yes, ma’am.”

Mrs. Jefferson resumed her seat.

“I’m not sure what you want to know,” she said. “Thomas signed up as soon as he could. He had this notion, Lord knows where he got it from, that he’d be fighting side by side with regular soldiers, white soldiers. But that isn’t what happened. He was disappointed, let me tell you. Bitterly disappointed. But he was assigned to a unit, the 761st Tank Battalion, and he was proud of that once he got through the training and was sent overseas.”

“He hated the training.” Daniel was still hovering in the kitchen doorway.

“I warned you, young man,” Mrs. Jefferson said.

“What didn’t he like about it?” I asked.

“It does no good to dwell on the past.” Mrs. Jefferson turned to Daniel. “And you weren’t even born yet, so anything you have to say is pure speculation on your part.”

“No it isn’t. I read every single letter he wrote. I read them over and over.”

"If you don't mind, Mrs. Jefferson, I'd like to hear what Daniel has to say."

Mrs. Jefferson sighed and shook her head. She waved him over and sat back to listen.

"They trained in Louisiana, for one thing," he said. "Bad as it is here—"

"Those days are past, Daniel." Mrs. Jefferson's tone was firm.

Daniel didn't argue with her, but I sensed his disagreement so strongly that he seemed to vibrate with it.

"You ever been down south?" he asked me. I shook my head.

"Neither have you," Mrs. Jefferson said mildly.

"I can read, can't I? I hear what they say on TV. TJ signed up thinking he'd be a soldier just like anyone else. But that didn't happen. Whites got trained and deployed and sent overseas in a couple of months. TJ had to spend two years training. Two years! And that wasn't the worst of it. Those crackers from some of the other army bases down there made trouble. One time they beat up a bunch of guys from TJ's unit. They even killed a man. But do you think anyone was arrested for that? No way! TJ said there was a quick investigation, and then the white unit that started the trouble got shipped out. You read the letter, Ma."

Ma? I looked from him to Mrs. Jefferson. Daniel must have noticed.

"TJ was my brother," he said.

"I remarried some time after Thomas's father, my first husband, died," Mrs. Jefferson said.

Daniel snorted. "Died? That's the way you talk about him? He died?"

Mrs. Jefferson shot him a warning glance.

"Do you want to stay or do you want to go, Daniel?" Her voice shook with anger. She and Daniel stared at each other until Daniel muttered a grudging, "Sorry, Ma."

"It's true that the training wasn't what Thomas expected," Mrs. Jefferson said. "But once he got overseas, things were different. Thomas distinguished himself. His unit was so good that General Patton himself asked to have it transferred to his command. He said the 761st was one of the best tank units he'd ever had the privilege to command. Those were General Patton's own words."

"You must have been proud of Thomas," I said.

Mrs. Jefferson smiled fondly, a faraway look in her eyes. "I was, and I am. Nothing will ever change that."

"He should have got a medal," Daniel said. "He should have got a bunch of them. But none of them did. The army kept all the medals for the white soldiers."

"Now, Daniel," Mrs. Jefferson cautioned.

I felt a pang in my heart when I looked across the table at her. I imagined her pride at her son in his crisp new uniform. I could almost see her waiting for the postman to pass by the chipped and dented mailbox at the end of her front walk. I pictured her sitting where she was right now, reading her son's letters for a second or even third time.

I imagined his return after the war like a little scene in my head: Mrs. Jefferson coming out onto her porch at the sound of a car engine and seeing her son standing there. Mrs. Jefferson running to him, arms outflung, smile wide, and catching him in her lean, strong arms. Catching her son and hugging him almost to death, so pleased was she to have him back and all in one piece. At least, I assumed he was all in one piece. No one had mentioned anything different.

"I bet you gave him a real homecoming," I said.

"I sure did. I cooked his favorite foods. I baked three pies. It took Thomas and Patrice all of two days to finish them."

"Patrice?" Was that the Frenchman Mr. Standish and the others had told me about, the murder victim?

"Thomas brought a friend home with him."

"From France," I said.

She shook her head. "From Canada. He was French-speaking, but he was from Canada. He spoke English too."

Canada? Something caught in my throat. I could barely breathe. Thomas Jefferson's friend was a Canadian. Was that why I was here? Was that where the newspaper picture was leading me—to a Canadian, like myself? To my—I hardly dared think it—father?

I shook the thought from my head. Suppose—just for a second, suppose—that it was true, that this murdered Canadian was my father. So what? He was dead, wasn't he? Killed by a friend, by someone he trusted, someone who was going to be his business partner—and over what?

Over some stupid thing someone else said? According to what the old men had told me, Mr. Jefferson had confessed to killing the Canadian because he expected his friend to stick up for him and he didn't. But there could be any number of reasons for that, couldn't there, for someone not sticking up for someone else? LaSalle was new in town. He didn't have the history to understand what was going on. Or maybe Mr. Jefferson had behaved badly. Maybe he had a raging temper. The way he'd been treated when he returned home wasn't fair, but Mrs. Hazelton always said that no matter how unfair a situation, you had to act in a civilized manner. Maybe Mr. Jefferson hadn't done that. Maybe his temper or his pride had got the better of him.

Or maybe LaSalle hadn't stuck up for Jefferson for other reasons. Maybe he had seemed like a good guy, but he turned out not to be the kind of guy who would stand up to a stranger in a strange town. You never know about people. You never know what they're going to do. Just because a man had been a soldier, that didn't mean he was brave. Sometimes you didn't realize that until it hit you over the head. Like when the person you were sure would tell his mother to go jump in the lake rather than let her dictate who he could and could not see ends up breaking *your* heart instead. Some people get angry when that happens. Some people cry.

"What was he like?" I asked Mrs. Jefferson. "Mr. LaSalle, I mean."

"Patrice was a nice man," she said. "He was different from most of the people in these parts. He stayed in this very house the whole time he was here. I know for a fact that some people in town said something to him about it, but it didn't bother him one bit."

"What do you mean, *they said something to him*?" I asked.

"They warned him," Daniel said.

His mother shot him another look. "You were no more than a baby. How do you know what anyone said to anyone else?"

"I live here, don't I?" Daniel looked defiantly back at her. "I've heard about what happened. Everyone's heard. And everyone says that TJ's *friend*"—he spat out the word—"would be alive if he'd listened to what people told him. If you ask me, TJ would be alive too."

My pulse quickened. "What do you mean?"

"Nothing," Mrs. Jefferson said hurriedly. "Nothing that makes any sense anyway." Her eyes narrowed, and she regarded me closely. "Why are you asking all these questions? What does any of this have to do with you?"

"I'm writing a story about it." I started telling her what I had told almost everyone else—but stopped before I had gone far. She had invited me into her home. She had answered my questions. It didn't seem right to lie to her. I started again. "A woman—the headmistress at my school..." I know. Mrs. Hazelton wasn't a headmistress and the Home wasn't a school, but I didn't feel comfortable telling anyone everything, not until I knew what everything was. "She gave me this." I pulled the clipping from my pocket and gave it to Mrs. Jefferson. She looked at it. Tears welled up in her eyes.

"They said he tried to escape from prison. They said they had no choice, they had to shoot him."

"In the back," Daniel said.

"This woman—my headmistress—told me that it's possible if I found out all about this picture, it might mean something to me."

Mrs. Jefferson looked up. "What could any of this possibly mean to you?"

"I don't know. But I sure would like to find out. I came all the way down here to see if I could."

Mrs. Jefferson peered into my eyes. I don't know exactly what she saw, but it was enough to start her talking again.

"You asked me about Patrice. I liked him. He was a good man."

Daniel grunted and shook his head in disgust. He wheeled around and left the kitchen. The screen door clattered shut behind him. Mrs. Jefferson didn't comment.

"He insisted on helping with the dishes every night," she continued. "He did yard work, too, and looked after Daniel if I had chores. It was like he was born to hold a baby in his arms. I've never seen a man take to a small child so fast. I didn't have to explain anything to him."

"Was he married?"

"Married?" Mrs. Jefferson smiled. "He was just a boy when he went overseas. Eighteen."

"So he wasn't married?"

"No."

"Did he mention a girlfriend back home? Or a fiancée? Or someone special?"

"The only thing I remember for sure is that he said he wished he could meet a nice girl and settle down and have a family. He liked children. I could tell by the way he played with the baby—with Daniel—that he wanted children of his own."

Eighteen was plenty old enough to be a father. That much I knew. I'd heard about it all my life: foolish girls who gave themselves over to callow boys and ended up with babies that filled orphanages all over the country. I'd been warned too. We'd all been warned, regularly, to mind our passions, to refuse to be fooled by all the things boys might say when their ardor (as Mrs. Hazelton called it) got the better of them. *It's up to you, girls*, she said. *You have the power to say no. And remember, if you say no and he gets angry, that tells you all you need to know about his character. A good boy—a gentleman—will always respect a lady's wishes, and you, my dear girls, despite what anyone else might think, despite what you yourselves might think, are all ladies.*

Which meant that it was possible—it was always possible—that Patrice LaSalle had left a baby behind in the belly or the arms of some girl when he went overseas. But if he had, it wasn't me, because that child, if she existed, would have been born before the war. She'd be much older than I was.

Or maybe he met someone overseas.

Or someone here.

That last thought caught in my mind. Patrice LaSalle could have come here with Thomas Jefferson and met someone right here in Freemount or in Orrenstown. Maybe that had caused trouble between them. Maybe that's why Mrs. Hazelton had saved that newspaper photo all this time. Maybe it was the clue. And maybe Thomas Jefferson had killed my father over a girl.

I drew in a deep breath.

"Did Mr. LaSalle date anyone when he was here?"

Mrs. Jefferson shook her head. "He and Thomas spent all their time making plans. They wanted to buy that garage out there. They had money saved up from their pay while they were overseas. Patrice was a good mechanic. They were sure they could make a go of it."

"Didn't Mr. LaSalle want to go home? Didn't he have family in Canada?"

"If he did, he was in no rush to see them," Mrs. Jefferson said. "But I got the impression there was no one back there for him. I remember he said that he was raised by his grandparents. He talked about his grandfather—his *granpear*, he called him. The way he talked about that old man, I know he loved him. And he said something about the special meat pies his grandmother made at Christmas. He had some French name for them, but I can't remember what it was."

Tourtière. She meant tourtière. People in Quebec make them at Christmastime. I learned that in school.

"I believe his grandfather died while he was overseas. I know for a fact his grandmother passed away before that. He never mentioned any other family."

Was it possible that Patrice LaSalle had been an orphan like me? If so, what had happened to his parents? How old was he when he went to live with his grandparents? At least he hadn't ended up in an orphanage. However few in number, he had other family members—and a family history. His grandfather had probably told him about Patrice's parents, and maybe about his great-grandparents too. His grandmother had probably done the same. He knew where he had come from. He'd never been stumped when someone asked him who his people were. He had a family tree and real roots. But those roots had nothing to do with mine, that much now seemed certain. He'd been a young man when he died—was murdered. There was no special girl in his life. No one to make a daughter with. Patrice LaSalle was a dead end. Anger and frustration roiled in my stomach. I'd been hoping that I was getting close, and now it looked like I was as far from the truth as I had ever been.

So what did the clipping mean? If my father wasn't Thomas Jefferson or Patrice LaSalle, whom did that leave? Whoever had desecrated Mr. Jefferson's grave? That would be some story. My father the Klansman.

I finished the last of my lemonade and thanked Mrs. Jefferson. I also apologized if I had stirred up sad memories. She smiled softly.

"Thomas was a good boy. I still don't know what you were hoping to find, but I can tell you this: my Thomas never killed anyone. He wasn't that kind of man." She raised a hand as if to fend off a protest it hadn't occurred to me to make. "I know they say he did it. They say he confessed. But that's not true. He told me so himself, the one time they let me see him. He said he didn't do it. Said he didn't confess either. But that old sheriff, the one who arrested him, got up in court and laid his hand on the Bible and swore an oath that everything coming out of his mouth was the truth, the whole truth and nothing but the truth."

Her face hardened, and she snorted with contempt. She got up for another glass and poured herself a little lemonade. She drank it before she continued. "He sat right there in that witness box and told the court that Thomas confessed what he did. He said criminals like Thomas—my boy, a criminal!—always felt the need to confess their crimes sooner or later, and that's what Thomas did. He said Thomas called him to his cell late one night after being plagued with nightmares and confessed to the murder. But the next day, the sheriff said, when he asked Thomas to put his confession in writing, he refused. I remember the exact words the sheriff said. He said that Thomas's heart hardened when the sun came up and he denied everything he had said the night before. He said he wasn't surprised about that, either, because Thomas had been a soldier, and soldiers are trained to kill without remorse. He said that was the price society paid for the democracy we all enjoyed."

She let out another snort. "Democracy! My son was sent to prison for a murder he didn't commit, thanks to the sheriff's lies, and he has the nerve to talk about democracy!"

I was taken aback by Mrs. Jefferson's vehemence, even though I saw how things were around here—the way people talked about Thomas and Freemount. From what Daniel had said, things hadn't improved for Thomas when he joined up. His dreams of being a soldier as good as any other were dashed. So were his hopes of being treated with respect when he returned home. It must have been hard for him. If he was angry about it, well, I could understand that. How many times had I punched a wall after suffering the looks of some of the women back home in Hope? And when Mrs. Danforth had me fired because she didn't think orphans should be trusted...I'd wanted to hurt her like she'd hurt me, only worse.

Still, Mr. Jefferson had been convicted of murder. He'd been sent to prison. That meant something, didn't it? People didn't get sent to prison for things they didn't do—did they?

Chapter Eleven

I FOLLOW A NEW LEAD

DANIEL WAS ON his knees weeding the garden again when I left the house. He glanced up when I came out the front door, but he didn't say anything. I watched him for a minute. I wanted to talk to him, but I saw the knot of tension in his back and the stiffness in his shoulders and felt his anger as he ripped weeds from around pink geraniums.

"The trial transcript is missing," I said. "The transcript from your brother's trial."

He didn't react.

"I went to the courthouse and asked for it. But it's gone. The clerk there said he had no idea what happened to it."

Still nothing.

"I'm staying at Miss Nearing's rooming house. You know her? She runs the newspaper. Her father ran it before her. He covered the trial. The newspaper picture I showed you came from Mr. Nearing's newspaper. But when I went looking for articles about the trial, I couldn't find anything.

All the newspapers from that time are missing. Miss Nearing says she doesn't know what happened to them. And there's nothing in the newspaper files either. It's all gone."

Daniel stood up and spun around.

"Seems like there's all kinds of stuff missing from that newspaper," he said, his whole body tense with anger.

"What do you mean?"

He gave me the once-over and then dismissed me.

"Never mind."

"Don't you think it's a pretty big coincidence that everything to do with your brother's arrest and trial has vanished?" I asked.

Silence hung between us like a curtain.

"He filed an appeal," Daniel said at last.

"Oh?"

"The lawyer he had for the trial, he was no good."

"What do you mean?" More to the point, how did *he* know? Daniel was a toddler when his brother died.

"He was my brother. I grew up here. I spent my whole life listening to people talk about him. You think I didn't want to find out everything I could about what happened? But Ma, she never wanted to talk about it. I used to ask her about TJ. It made her cry every time. After a while I stopped asking her and started listening to what other people were saying. Mostly, it wasn't anything I wanted to hear. Everyone in town"—he gestured with his head—"says he did it. No wonder Ma cried all the time." He looked me in the eye. "There was an old man—he was old at the time of the trial.

Ezekiel Washington. He was the janitor at the courthouse. When I was twelve, our class did a field trip to the courthouse. It was supposed to teach us all about what a great system we have here, how justice is impartial and blind, all that stuff." He gave a twist to a lot of the words he spat out, like *great* and *impartial* and *blind*. "Mr. Washington was emptying the wastebaskets in the courtroom we were in, and when Mrs. White, my teacher, gave her little speech about justice being blind, I heard a sound, like a snort. We all did. We all looked at Ezekiel. Mrs. White knew he'd made the noise, but he looked at her as if he couldn't think where the sound came from. She gave him the evil eye. You should have seen her. She was from Mississippi. The only reason she was up here is that she married a farmer here. A pig farmer. She tried to act like we were all the same, but you could tell she didn't like having me and some of the others in her class."

"What others?"

Daniel gave me a withering look. "She was used to segregated schools. But they haven't had segregated schools in this state since 1949. She didn't like having me in her class. And she didn't like hearing that sound. She asked Ezekiel if he'd made it. He told her, *No, ma'am*, polite as pie. When she looked away, he winked at me. As we were leaving, he asked me my name. When I told him, he asked was I related to Thomas Jefferson. I said yes. It was the end of the day. Mrs. White had already dismissed us. So I stayed a while to talk to him. He was the one who told me that TJ's lawyer was no good."

"What did he say?"

"That the lawyer was assigned by the court. That he didn't raise a single objection during the whole trial. That he barely asked any questions. And that Ezekiel could see that TJ wasn't happy with that. He said one time TJ had to elbow his lawyer to get him to wake up. He'd dozed off right there in court!"

"Why didn't he hire a new lawyer?"

"He couldn't find one in time. The trial began while he was still looking. He wanted to get a lawyer from New York City, from Harlem, who was supposed to be really good. But the trial started before TJ heard back from him, and it was over fast because nobody objected to the sheriff's testimony about the confession. The jury took all of ten minutes to reach a verdict. Guilty. That's what Ezekiel told me. TJ was sent to prison. While he was in there, he tried to get another lawyer. But they made it hard for him. He wrote letters but never heard back. He told Ma that he thought they weren't mailing his letters like they were supposed to. He tried to get her to smuggle out some letters, but they searched her when she left, and they confiscated them. So he did the best he could in the prison library. He was trying to put together an appeal."

"What happened?"

"You already know what happened. He got shot while supposedly escaping."

I was beginning to think that something bad had taken place in Orrenstown. White people in town had told me how much TJ was resented, that they didn't like the way he strutted, as they put it, and refused to step aside. They didn't like the way he thought he was equal to them. But I was getting a different story from Mrs. Jefferson and Daniel. TJ had joined the army because he wanted to serve his country. But instead of being treated like everyone else, he found that the prejudice he'd faced all his life had followed him into basic training. It was still there when he returned home after the war with a white friend. When I put together everything I had discovered so far—and added to the mix the fact that every single record related to the murder and the trial had somehow disappeared—it wasn't hard to at least suspect that someone else might have killed Mr. LaSalle and that somehow Mr. Jefferson had been railroaded for it. It was a great story. Okay, so it wasn't the story I had set out to write. But I bet if Nellie Bly had stumbled on it, she wouldn't have let it go until she got to the bottom of it. That pretty much made up my mind.

"Where can I find Mr. Washington?"

Daniel's smile was wry as he nodded in the direction of the cemetery.

"Oh," I said when I understood his meaning. Another dead end. Always another dead end. I looked at Daniel and thought about what he had just said. "*Supposedly* escaping?"

"TJ wasn't stupid."

"But you were just—"

"A kid when it happened? I know. Ma keeps telling me. If I hear it one more time..." He paused and took a deep breath to calm himself. "I'm not stupid either. When I was a kid, there were pictures of TJ all over the house." I didn't remember seeing any during my brief visit. "Over the years, Ma took them down. She never said so, but I think it hurt her too much to look at them."

I could see that. It was plain from everything Mrs. Jefferson had said and from the soft way she said his name that she still loved him fiercely.

"I would stare at those pictures and pester Ma for information about him. But she would never tell me very much—except that he was my brother and a war hero and he died and was buried out in the cemetery. If you look out Ma's bedroom window, you'll see the gravestone." He nodded toward it. "I was like most kids. I was curious. But when I started asking people, I heard all kinds of stories. Black people, like Ezekiel, they told me that TJ would never have killed anyone, that they didn't believe it. White people—the ones in this town anyway—they all said it was true. It had to be true because he confessed and because a jury decided he was guilty. But they can't both be right."

"Did you find out what really happened?"

"I *know* what really happened. My brother didn't kill that man. He had no reason to." Before I could open my mouth to say anything—and I wasn't sure I was even going to—he said, "I know what *they* say. I've heard it all. But I don't believe it."

"Someone told me that there were witnesses to an argument between your brother and Mr. LaSalle."

"There was *a* witness. One. And he was white. He didn't like TJ."

He was right about that.

"There must be someone else who saw what happened," I said.

"If there is, I don't know who it is. But I'll tell you what. I'm not at all surprised that those courthouse files are missing. It fits with what I've been telling you." He picked up the watering can.

"What about your brother's grave?"

"What about it?"

"Someone vandalized it."

"That was a long time ago."

"Do you have any idea who did it?"

"Ma says it was likely some ignorant fool."

"Do you know why they did it? Was there any kind of message? Or threat?"

"Not that I know of. If there was, Ma never said." He tipped the can to water the flowers. "I guess now you'll go back to wherever you came from."

"Maybe," I said. But even as I spoke, I knew that I wasn't going anywhere.

The sun was hammering the asphalt, sending waves of burning heat up my ankles and calves and parching my throat. There wasn't a cloud in the sky. Nothing moved;

there wasn't even a breath of breeze. As I hiked back to Orrenstown, all I could think about was Mrs. Jefferson's ice-cold lemonade. I would have done just about anything for another glass of that, with chunks of ice floating in it. But it wasn't going to happen. It reminded me of chaperoned trips into Hope when I was little. It was always a treat to walk into town with one of the older girls. A treat and torture because going into town meant walking by Loretta's Diner and smelling the freshly baked crullers that I had no money to buy. It meant stopping in front of the Orpheus to see what was playing but never having the money to go inside and watch a movie. In summer, it meant seeing kids strolling with their parents—parents!—licking double-scoop ice-cream cones. Sometimes it had seemed that stepping beyond the fence surrounding the Home meant being reminded of all the things that were forever out of my reach.

I did now what I used to force myself to do then: I thought about something else. I kept walking.

I wondered how the others were doing, especially Malou, who had at least one parent who was black. She had no idea which one. I wondered where she was and what she was doing, and whether she'd run into any of the prejudice I'd seen here. It would be personal for her. At the orphanage, she was treated like everyone else. But out here in the real world... Meeting up with what I'd witnessed so far could change everything in Malou's life.

I thought, too, about Mr. Jefferson. I couldn't figure out what he had to do with me. For one fleeting moment I had thought—even hoped—that Patrice LaSalle was my father, that even though I had missed the chance to meet him, and he himself had no family left, I at least would have had some idea of where I'd come from and maybe some possibility of finding out more about my father's family. I might even—and this was the hardest dream to conjure and then give up on—have been able to find out who my mother was. She might still be alive. Children got put in orphanages for lots of reasons, not just because they were orphans. There were girls at the Home whose mothers had had no choice but to give them up. Girls whose mothers hadn't been married. Girls whose mothers had done shameful things that led to babies being born. Unwanted babies. Bastard babies. Babies that were looked down on by people, unless and until they were adopted into proper families and given proper names, until and unless their old selves, their original selves, were erased and they were given new identities. Lucky girls, for the most part, although we had all heard stories—rumors, really—about girls being adopted and then treated as housemaids. Unhappy girls whose dreams of a real family had been dashed. Girls who soon wished they were back in the Home.

But that was in the past now. My life was finally my own to shape, the way a potter shapes a bowl. It was mine to fill however I wanted. *We are all vessels*, Mrs. Hazelton said. *And we all decide what we will carry within ourselves. Will we carry love or hate? Compassion or disdain? Charity or selfishness? Hope or despair? Justice or injustice?* I used to tune out when she launched into her little sermons, which she usually did when she invited the seven of us to her study to sip tea and nibble biscuits like ladies. Now I saw what she meant. The people in Orrenstown were vessels too. Some of them had filled themselves with prejudice and hatred. Others, like Mrs. Jefferson, overflowed with love and longing. And what about me? I had come down here looking for my past. Maybe I would find it, and maybe I wouldn't. But I had the feeling that I might discover something else. Something that could change my life. Launch me on my dream. It's what Nellie Bly had done. She started by speaking out for women and against the limitations imposed on us. She broadened out from there, seeking out injustice and shining a journalistic light on it. She made a difference. Maybe I could make a difference too. And write one heck of a good story.

But how was I going to get the facts? The newspaper coverage was missing. The newspaper files were missing. The court records were missing. Where else could I look for information?

The sheriff's office.

There had to be something at the sheriff's office. The sheriff had arrested Mr. Jefferson. Not Sheriff Hicks, but the one before him. There had to be police records and files.

I picked up my pace despite the heat and my thirst, and finally—hallelujah!—I saw buildings on the horizon. I stopped at a grocery store and bought a bottle of soda, half of which I downed on the spot in one long, unladylike gulp. I sipped the rest as I followed the cashier's directions to the sheriff's office at the far end of the street. It was a small brick building with a cornerstone that had been laid in 1903. I went inside and approached a counter that divided the room in half. A few desks stood on the other side. All but one was empty. A woman sat at that desk. She looked like a secretary, with her neat pearls and twinset, and she was on the phone. Another woman, a black woman, pushed a cleaning cart between the two rows of desks. She stopped at the windows, pulled out a bottle of cleaner and began to spray the windows. The woman on the phone glanced at me and held up a finger. She dispatched her caller quickly, removed her eyeglasses and asked if I needed help.

"I'd like to speak to Sheriff Hicks."

"Is he expecting you?"

"No. But he knows me." I gave her my name.

The woman looked me over. "You're that girl everyone is talking about, aren't you?"

Really? *Everyone* was talking about me?

"You're the one who's been asking about Tom Jefferson," the woman said.

"Did you know him?"

"I didn't live here at the time. But I've heard about him."

I wondered which story she had heard.

"I really need to speak to Sheriff Hicks," I said.

The woman hesitated a moment but finally picked up the phone and punched a button. She kept her voice low as she spoke into the mouthpiece. She hung up and said, "He'll be right out."

Sure enough, a door opened at the back of the room, and Sheriff Hicks appeared. He smiled when he saw me.

"What can I do for you, young lady?"

I glanced at the woman. She was leaning forward over her desk, all ears.

"Can I talk to you for a minute? In private?"

Sheriff Hicks raised a flap in the counter to let me through. He guided me to his office and closed the door. "What's on your mind?"

"It's about Thomas Jefferson."

He shook his head.

"You've got tongues wagging all over town, young lady." He sank down on the chair behind his desk and fixed me with a steady gaze. "I think it's time to level with me, Miss Cady Andrews. What really brings you to town?"

"I already told you. I'm just—"

"Writing some kind of a story before you head home to New York. Is that it?"

I nodded.

"And here you are in my office, asking about something that happened when you were a tiny baby. People are talking. And what with all the trouble that's happening down south..." His voice trailed off, and he shook his head again, his eyes on me the whole time.

"I already said I'm not here to make trouble." Except I wasn't so sure anymore, not after talking to Mrs. Jefferson and Daniel.

"Uh-huh." He eyed me speculatively. "Those kids that went down to Mississippi, they're a lot like you. College kids. There are hundreds of them down there trying to get colored folks to register to vote. It's stirring up a lot of bad feelings, let me tell you, all those outsiders mixing in where they're not wanted. Some of those kids have come smack up against Mississippi tradition. Some of them have been hospitalized. I wouldn't be the least bit surprised if someone was killed down there this summer. People are wondering if you're one of them, if you're part of the plan, showing up here and asking a bunch of questions about a colored fella."

"I have nothing to do with anything that's happening in Mississippi. And anyway, people have a right to vote, don't they?"

"If that's what they want to do. They also have a right to be left alone if they don't care to vote. They have a right not to be harassed by a bunch of college kids who don't know what they're talking about and who listen to people who don't know what they're talking about either. Not to mention people who make their living by stirring things up. Professional agitators." He leaned back in his chair. "What is it that you want to ask me?"

"Can I see the police file on Thomas Jefferson? I'd also like to see anything you have on Patrice LaSalle."

He studied me for a few seconds.

"First you ask about the Jefferson boy and what he did. Now you want to know about the fella he murdered. Care to tell me what your real interest is in that case?"

I repeated what I'd told him when I first met him. "I heard about it. I got curious. I think it would make a good story."

"For your school paper?"

"Maybe."

"You know what they say about curiosity."

"I know what they say it does to cats," I told him. "But I'm not a cat. So, can I please see the files?"

"No, you cannot." Before I could ask why not, he continued. "In the first place, police files are not open to the public. Second, those files no longer exist. This isn't the original sheriff's office. The original one was flooded out."

"And the records?"

"Ruined."

Dead end. Again.

"You didn't happen to be working here at the time of the murder, did you, Sheriff Hicks?"

"I was here," he said. My heart sped up. "But I wasn't involved in the investigation. The sheriff took care of that himself."

"But you're familiar with the case—with what happened?"

"I know the broad strokes."

"Can you tell me about it—about what you know?"

He sighed. "You're persistent, I'll give you that. But there's no advantage to digging into the past, especially that particular slice of it, particularly not now, when people are already worked up about what's happening down in Mississippi. You don't want to go stirring up all kinds of bad memories, do you? Besides, aren't your folks missing you? Don't you think you should head home?" He stood up.

The message was clear: he wasn't going to answer my question.

The woman who was washing windows looked over her shoulder at me when I left Sheriff Hicks's office. So did the woman at the desk. Her eyes stayed on me as I walked across the room. I glanced at her as I closed the door behind me. She was on her way to the sheriff's office. The gossip train was rolling on.

Chapter Twelve

ANOTHER FIRE

I WENT FROM the sheriff's office to the drugstore, where I bought a *New York Times*. I took it back to Maggie's and sat on the porch to read it. So far, no one had found the three civil rights workers who had gone missing in Mississippi.

The screen door opened.

"Well, I was wondering where you'd disappeared to." It was Maggie. She glanced at the paper. "Checking out the news from back home?"

I couldn't remember telling her where I was from. So how did she know? Who had she been talking to?

"I got a call from the courthouse." She sat down in a wicker chair. "One of the clerks wanted to know why I was interested in the Thomas Jefferson murder trial." I felt my cheeks redden. I couldn't even look at her. "The funny thing is, I have no interest in it. So I asked him what he was talking about, and do you know what he said?"

I had a pretty good idea. "He said someone was in there looking for the transcript. He said it was a girl and that she gave my name."

"I'm sorry." I was too. Genuinely sorry. "But he wasn't going to help me until I mentioned you and the newspaper."

Maggie appraised me for longer than felt comfortable. "I told him I was kicking around a few story ideas about war veterans and how they fare when they get home," she said at last. "We have quite a few who were over in Korea too. Some haven't done well. But it would have been nice if you'd told me what you were up to. I had to think pretty fast, let me tell you." She ducked her head so that she could look me in the eye. "Why are you so interested in Thomas Jefferson? And why are you telling everyone you're from New York when clearly you're not?"

My head snapped up at that. "How did—"

She raised a hand to silence me.

"I spent a few years in New York, Cady. I know what people there look like and sound like. You're not from there. In fact, unless I miss my guess, you're from Canada. I can hear it in the way you speak."

I stared at her. For once I didn't know what to say.

"Time to come clean, young lady."

She didn't have to ask twice. I told her everything. Maybe that old sheriff had been right when he told Mrs. Jefferson that people who'd done something wrong really needed to confess to feel better. I told her about Mrs. Hazelton and the envelope. I also told her about Mr. Travers and the *Weekly Crier* and about the story I hoped to write and why it was so important to me. She didn't laugh. She didn't make fun of me. Instead she smiled and said, "Reporter, huh? It's a tough row to hoe for a woman. But it can be done, Cady. It really can. I started on a newspaper in San Francisco. I had to fight long and hard to get decent assignments, and by that I mean real news, not the women's pages, although I paid my dues there. I covered social events just like you did. I did a recipe column for a while. I wrote about hairstyles and fashion and how to feed a family of six on just pennies a day." She sighed. "I thought I was doomed to a lifetime of non-news—at a newspaper, no less!"

"Is that why you came back here?"

She shook her head.

"There was a murder—a woman killed her husband. I had met the woman once before, and when the reporters came clamoring for a story about the Black Widow—that's what one of the rival newspapers called her—she refused to talk to them. She refused to talk to anyone except me. My editor had no choice. I got the story. I told her side."

"But she killed her husband."

"In self-defense. He was a gambler and a drinker—most of the other papers didn't report that. I dug into his life. I painted a portrait of the man. My publisher got a lot of flak—how dare I say it was the husband's fault he was murdered? But my editor stuck with me. And because my stories were selling papers, the publisher came around.

I covered the trial from start to finish. By the time the jury acquitted her, I had proved myself. My editor moved me from the women's pages to hard news. I caught some big stories there. Crime. Corruption. Crooked politicians. You name it. I had the time of my life. But it was hard work. All I ever did was chase stories. I felt like I had no other life."

Her smile had more sad than happy in it. "I thought I wanted a change, so when my father died, I came back here. Did I tell you my grandfather started the paper? It's been in the family for three generations—four, now that I'm here. But I'm afraid I'll be the end of the line. And I've been wondering if I did the right thing by coming here. It's quiet—maybe a little too quiet." She sighed. "So, what's going on, Cady?"

"I don't think Mr. Jefferson killed Mr. LaSalle." There. I'd said it. The thought had been spinning around in my brain ever since I'd spoken to Daniel and Mrs. Jefferson. Maybe since before that. Maybe since I'd found out that almost every scrap of information about the trial was missing. "I want to find out. I want to write about it as badly as you wanted to tell that woman's side of the story." But there was a problem. I would have to tell her sooner or later. I decided on right now. "I'm not sure I can afford to stay on with you, Maggie."

"If you don't stay here, I don't know where you'll go. This is the only place in town besides the hotel. And that hotel is no place for a young girl. It attracts mostly traveling salesmen. Besides, it's expensive. I'll tell you what.

You can do chores in return for your room and board for as long as you're here."

"Are you sure? I don't know how long it will—"

"I'm sure." She stood up. "That's settled."

"I'm great at cleaning," I told her. "I've scrubbed more floors, washed more walls and polished more windows than you can imagine."

Maggie smiled. "I was going to hire a girl to do some cleaning. The place really needs it, and I don't have the time. I'm sure we can work something out." She paused as she opened the screen door. "Have you talked to Lorne Beale?"

"Who's he?"

"He was the sheriff back in the '40s. He'd be pretty old by now, but I know he's still around." She disappeared inside and was back in a flash with a slim telephone book. She thumbed through it. "Humph. He's not in here." I was pretty sure I heard disappointment in her voice. "Leave it with me. I'm sure I can track him down. Come on. Let's have some lunch."

Arthur was in the kitchen, slicing tomatoes. I washed the lettuce, and we all sat down to iced tea, tomato sandwiches and a crisp salad. After that, I got to work washing the floors of all the upstairs bedrooms. By the time I caught the first whiff of supper—it smelled like chicken (it was, with a big bowl of fresh peas)—I had worked up a real appetite.

It was just Maggie and me for supper. Arthur was working late.

"I found Lorne Beale," Maggie said casually. My heart slammed to a stop. Finally, a real honest-to-goodness lead! "He's in a nursing home over in Fairview."

"Where's that?"

"About fifteen miles north of here."

Fifteen *miles*?

"Is there a bus?"

"It just so happens that I have to drive to Fairview tomorrow. There's a man up there who can apparently whistle the whole of Beethoven's Fifth Symphony. Everyone says he's pretty good." She makes a wry face. "I know—it isn't exactly earth-shattering news. But I learned pretty quickly that local people are interested in local people—your Mr. Travers understands that, I'm sure. I'll drop you there on my way."

I heard thumping. Then hammering. Someone yelled, "Get up, get up!" I smelled smoke.

I was dreaming, and, of all things, I was dreaming of the Home. I never thought I would.

More thumping, only this time I was awake.

"Cady, come on! You have to get out of the house!"

I threw off my sheet and ran to the door.

"Come on," Maggie said.

We raced downstairs and out into the yard. A fire truck stood at the curb. Firemen were hosing down the front of the house where the parlor was.

"What happened?" I asked.

A fireman came down the front walk and stopped in front of Maggie.

"Looks like someone threw a homemade firebomb through your window." He held up the remains of a bottle. "It's a good thing you were home and awake when it happened. It was filled with gasoline. Fire's out. I don't think there's any structural damage, but we'll have to get the fire marshal down to take a look first thing in the morning."

Another car pulled up, and Sheriff Hicks got out. The fireman went to report to him. When he was finished, Sheriff Hicks walked over to Maggie and me.

"Bert says someone threw a Molotov cocktail through your window," he said. "You have any idea why someone would do that?"

I looked apprehensively at Maggie. How would she answer?

"No idea at all." Maggie's voice was shaky. She was rattled, and I didn't blame her. What if she hadn't woken up? What if the fire had spread more quickly? What if someone had been hurt? Maggie looked around. "Where's Arthur?" Her voice rose with panic. "Arthur?" she called. "Arthur?"

"Over here!" Arthur was at the side of the house with a group of firemen.

"Are you sure no one has a grudge against you?" Sheriff Hicks asked, looking directly at me.

"I'm pretty sure," Maggie said. "You read the paper, Brad. Have you seen anything in there that would offend anyone or make anyone angry at me?"

Sheriff Hicks had to admit that he hadn't.

"But someone sure sent you a message," he said. "Either that or we've got an arsonist on the loose. I'll be back with the fire marshal first thing in the morning." He glanced at me. "Can I have a word with you in private, Maggie?"

Maggie obliged. She and the sheriff crossed the street to his parked car and stood there talking. I couldn't hear what they were saying, but I saw Maggie shake her head again and again. When she finally returned, she said, "He wanted to know if I thought you had anything to do with it."

What? "He thinks *I* started the fire?"

"He thinks all your questions about Thomas Jefferson are getting people riled up. He says everyone is talking about what's going on in Mississippi, and they think it's peculiar that you showed up here at the same time and started looking into Jefferson's murder trial. He says you've been seen in Freemount."

"Is that a crime?"

"Not that I know of. But it's not the usual thing for people to do around here."

Chapter Thirteen

I HIT A DEAD END...AND FIND A NEW LINE OF INQUIRY

THE NEXT MORNING, after we'd spent the night in a neighbor's front room, the fire marshal confirmed that the damage was superficial. Maggie heaved a sigh of relief. She and I drove up to Fairview while Arthur nailed plywood over the broken parlor windows, which would have to do until Maggie could get them replaced.

The nursing home that housed Lorne Beale, the former sheriff, was a low-slung building surrounded by a lush green lawn dotted with flower beds and rows of shrubbery. The windows twinkled in the late-morning sun. A bright-white sign with black letters set at the entrance to the driveway identified the place as *John H. Chisholm Home for the Aged.*

"Who was John H. Chisholm?" I asked.

"Is," Maggie said. "He's a very rich man. He owns a couple of canneries, two dairies, a trucking company and a tomato-processing plant. Inherited it all from his daddy. But he didn't turn out to be one of those second-generation born-with-a-silver-spoon-in-his-mouth types who only know how to spend money but not how to make it. He's wealthier than his father could ever have imagined. There's a rumor going around that he's planning to run for state governor." She nodded at the building as she pulled into the parking lot. "He also owns this nursing home."

"He owns it *and* he put his own name on it?"

"Thinks highly of himself, doesn't he? I hear it's a nice place. I've never been in it. I also hear that you need a lot more than what social security pays to stay here. Frankly, I'm surprised Sheriff Beale can afford it. Being sheriff might sound important, but the pay is strictly civil service." She leaned across me to open the passenger-side door. "I'll pick you up as soon as I snap a few pictures and hear a few bars of Beethoven's Fifth."

I jumped down and smoothed my skirt over my knees.

"Wish me luck," I said.

Maggie gave me a thumbs-up and put the truck into gear.

As soon as I stepped into the cool, bright foyer, a woman at the reception desk looked up.

"Can I help you?"

"I'm here to see Mr. Lorne Beale."

The woman smiled. "You must be his granddaughter. He used to talk about you all the time."

"Used to?" Past tense. I didn't like the sound of that. Had he died?

"He'll be thrilled to see you," the woman said.

I breathed a sigh of relief. He was still alive.

"Go down that hall." She pointed. "Make a left turn when you can't go straight anymore, and follow the corridor to the end. And don't worry."

"I beg your pardon?"

"I've seen a lot of grandchildren visit for the first time, and they all have that same look on their faces. They all expect it to be horribly depressing in here. But it's not. You'll see. And your grandfather has the best room in the house."

I thanked her and followed her directions. She was right. The place was far from depressing. It was flooded with light. Paintings, mostly still lifes, hung on the walls. When I turned at the end of the hall, I found a corner alcove with two large windows, a couple of comfortable chairs and a small table. People could sit here and talk while enjoying the view. If only there had been a nook like this at the orphanage, somewhere quiet to read or think. There was only one door at the end of the hall. I knocked and heard footsteps. Mr. Beale had a spritely step. I hoped he had as lively a mind.

The door opened.

It wasn't Mr. Beale. It was a woman in a starched white uniform and cap, with white stockings and matching crepe-soled shoes.

"Susan called and said you were on your way." She stood aside to let me in. "I'm Mrs. Cadogan, your grandfather's nurse."

I wanted to tell her I wasn't his granddaughter, but it seemed a little late for that. I followed her inside. Mr. Beale's room turned out to be two rooms, both larger than I had expected. The first was a sitting room with a hi-fi and a TV. The second was a bedroom, equipped with a hospital bed. An old man was lying in it, his head raised, his gray face lolling to one side, an oxygen mask strapped to his face. He stared at me. One eye drooped.

"Go on," Mrs. Cadogan said.

I approached the bed. The old man continued to stare at me.

"I'll be in the other room," Mrs. Cadogan said. "But I'll leave the door open in case you need me."

I went closer. One corner of Mr. Beale's mouth sagged under the oxygen mask.

"H—hello," I said softly. I glanced over my shoulder. Mrs. Cadogan was in the other room, watching a game show on TV.

"I need to ask you about Thomas Jefferson." I leaned closer so that I could speak into his ear. "Do you remember him?"

The old man's eyes narrowed. He opened his mouth, but all that came out were guttural sounds. I couldn't understand a word. I wasn't even sure they were words.

His grunting got louder. He raised one shaking hand to his face and tugged on his oxygen mask.

I called for Mrs. Cadogan. She rushed into the room and calmly but firmly removed Mr. Beale's hand from the mask and returned it to his side.

"Now, now, Mr. Beale. You know that has to stay where it is." She spoke quietly, in a soothing voice, and held his shoulders until he stopped struggling. “That’s it. Settle down. Look, your granddaughter is here.”

The old man closed his eyes. Mrs. Cadogan led me from the room.

“I am sorry, dear. I guess it’s too much excitement.”

“What...what happened to him?” I asked. “He was trying to say something to me, but I couldn’t understand him.”

“Didn’t your mother tell you? Honey, your grandfather had a stroke.”

“I didn’t know.”

“Well, I’m sorry to be the one to deliver the news. Since the stroke, your grandfather can’t talk. There’s a very good chance that he’ll never speak again. But that doesn’t mean you can’t talk to him. He understands what people say. Well, most of what people say. I think.”

“But how does he communicate with you?” I had an idea. “Can he write?”

Mrs. Cadogan shook her head. “I wish he could. He gets so frustrated when he tries to express himself.”

Poor old man. I couldn’t imagine how awful it must be to hear what is going on around you but have no way of making yourself heard or, even more important, understood.

“You will come back, won’t you?” Mrs. Cadogan pressed. “He’ll be so disappointed if you don’t.”

I told her I would. I felt bad, though, because I had no intention of returning. Mr. Beale wasn’t going to be able to help me.

I had to wait by the side of the road for a good fifteen minutes before Maggie returned to fetch me.

"So?" she asked as I slid into the front seat. "Did you find out anything?"

I told her what had happened.

"Well, I guess that was a dead end," Maggie said. "I'm sorry."

"How was the whistler?"

"You're going to laugh when I say this, but he was very good. I got a great picture for the front page."

The day was a complete write-off, or so I thought until I was doing the supper dishes. I heard the doorbell ring, and a minute later Maggie poked her head into the kitchen to tell me that I had a visitor.

"I do?" How was that even possible? I barely knew anyone in town.

There was no one in the front hall.

"He said he preferred to wait outside," Maggie told me.

I went out onto the porch. At first I didn't see anyone. Then something moved in the shadows.

"Daniel. What a surprise!"

Daniel nodded at the plywood over the parlor window.

"I heard about the fire. Ma wanted me to make sure you were all right."

"I'm fine. I feel bad for Maggie though."

"I heard it was arson."

"The fire marshal was here. And the sheriff. But so far there's no suspect."

"You think it happened because of you?"

"It crossed my mind, but I hope not." I told him about going to see Sheriff Hicks, who'd told me the police records had been destroyed, and then about my visit to the former sheriff. "He can't even talk." I was so discouraged. There had to be someone who knew what had happened all those years ago. "Daniel, do you know anyone who knew your brother? Anyone who's still alive, I mean."

"Besides Ma?"

I nodded.

"There's Edgar."

I recognized the name. "The caretaker from the church?"

"Yeah. He knew TJ. He still talks about him sometimes. Tells stories about him. When TJ was a kid, Edgar did odd jobs. He could fix anything. He also did gardening. Looked after people's properties. TJ used to help him."

"Do you think he'd talk to me? Do you know where he lives?"

"He has a place a couple of miles from here. But these days, mostly he's at the church. You want me to introduce you?"

I said yes, and we made plans to meet the next day.

I got up early the next morning and dusted and vacuumed the living room and dining room before breakfast.

"My goodness," Maggie said. "I didn't mean for you to do everything in one day." She spooned fluffy scrambled eggs onto my plate along with strips of crispy bacon and slices of golden toast. "Try the jam," she said. "I made it myself."

It was strawberry, filled with chunks of ruby-red fruit. It was the best jam I had ever tasted. I ate faster than I'd intended and then waited as patiently as I could for Maggie to finish so that I could tidy up.

"Go on," Maggie said with a laugh. "You look like you have ants in your pants." I was almost at the door when she added, "There's a bicycle in the garage. You can use it, if you want to."

The bike was old, and most of its original blue paint had chipped off, but it was well oiled, and the seat was thickly padded. I covered the distance between Orrenstown and Freemount in record time and found Daniel waiting at the road that led to the churchyard. I left my bike at the church's front door, and we went inside. The little church was a wood-framed structure with straight-backed plank pews. A dais took up most of the front of the church, and there was a podium to one side where the minister delivered his sermons. There was no organ, just a well-worn upright piano. Apart from a bare cross on the front wall, the place was unadorned. The windows were plain glass, although someone—Edgar?—had buffed them until they sparkled.

Edgar was mopping the vestry floor. He smiled and leaned on his mop handle when he saw Daniel and asked after his mother before turning to me with an expectant look on his face. Daniel introduced me.

"Cady wants to talk to you about TJ," he said.

Edgar's face clouded.

"What you want to know?"

"Daniel says you knew him well."

Edgar nodded. "He was a good boy. Worked with me after school most days. He was always looking to make a little extra money."

"What about when he came back after the war?"

"He didn't work for me then, if that's what you're asking. He had other plans. Came back here with a buddy, and the two of them talked about opening a garage."

"What I really want to know is what TJ did with his time after he came back."

"What he did with his time?" Edgar scratched his head. "He wasn't back all that long before..." He broke off. "I know he talked to Mr. Jenkins down at the bank about a loan. Must have done okay too, because he was busting all over with smiles that day. Oh, and he and that friend of his—what was his name now?"

"Patrice," Daniel said.

Edgar nodded. "Told me it was French for Patrick. The two of them liked to blow off steam. And who could blame them, two young men back from the war. They used to go down to the roadhouse. The joint was always jumping. Music, booze and lots of red-blooded American boys and girls."

"What roadhouse?" Daniel asked.

"You're too young to remember it. The place burned down in '49. It was no accident neither. Folks said it was burned on purpose."

"Why?" I asked.

"Story was that it was on account of the man who owned the place. They said he got himself in the middle of a liquor war. There was two rival suppliers of, well, let's call it non-government-approved liquid refreshment. One supplier was white, the other was black. The owner went with the black fella. The white fella—I think he was out of Indianapolis—didn't like his business being poached, so he arranged a fire. That's one story. It's the one the police settled on."

"Is there another story?" I asked.

"There is." Edgar's face grew more serious. "I never set foot in the place. I had my troubles with drink in the past, and I took the pledge. But I used to hear about that place. One thing I heard time and time again was that there were plenty of people in town"—he nodded in the direction of Orrenstown—"who didn't like the fact that their children were going down the road to a Negro establishment and were rubbing shoulders with colored folks, dancing to their lewd music—that's what the white preacher and the mayor and some of the others called it. There's plenty of people who think that's the real reason the place was burned."

"Do you know anyone who worked there?" I asked. "Maybe the owner?"

He shook his head. "He's long gone. Everyone is. The flood drove a lot of people away. Most people, in fact. Ain't anyone left from that place."

I thanked Edgar and waited while he and Daniel chatted. Finally Daniel said his goodbyes, and we left.

"I sure would like to know more about that roadhouse," I said.

"Why? What are you thinking?" Daniel asked.

"I don't know much about Orrenstown, but people seem upset about what's going on in Mississippi, and I've heard some people say that your brother didn't act the way they expected him to when he came back from overseas. People say he acted superior."

"He didn't *act* anything." Daniel's nostrils flared. "He was just a person. A man. And a soldier."

"If what Edgar said is true, if the roadhouse was burned down because people didn't like that white kids were hanging around down there, then maybe that has something to do with what happened to your brother."

"You think TJ got on the wrong side of some white boys?"

"I think it's possible."

Daniel thought for a minute. "Ma used to know everyone around here. Maybe she knows what happened to the owner of the roadhouse."

"Can you ask her?" I glanced at my watch. "I have to make a phone call. I have to check on something."

"Why do you want to write about my brother?"

"Because something is wrong. It's just too much of a coincidence that everything about the case is missing. And"—I hesitated, but not for long—"because I want to be a reporter, and I think this story might help me."

"A reporter?"

"Mrs. Hazelton—my headmistress—always used to say that we should set our sights high. Everyone else always told us to be grateful we had a roof over our heads. But Mrs. Hazelton says the reason we have dreams is to help us strive for something better. I'm striving to be a reporter. And Mrs. Hazelton says that just because something seems impossible now, that doesn't mean it will never happen."

"Ma says the same thing," Daniel said. "She worries a lot. She says life is unfair, especially for colored people. But she believes that can change. She thinks Mr. King has the right idea."

"Mr. King?"

"Mr. Reverend Martin Luther King Jr." Daniel told me about the bus boycott in Montgomery, Alabama, in 1955, when a black woman named Rosa Parks was arrested for refusing to give her seat to a white person. "She had worked all day, and she was tired. She didn't see why she should have to give up her seat when she paid her fare same as anyone else. A lot of people thought a boycott was useless and that it wouldn't get anywhere. But it ended with the Supreme Court ruling that segregated buses are unconstitutional. Reverend King was involved." Daniel spoke quickly, and his eyes were bright with excitement. "He also led a protest march in Birmingham, Alabama. The protesters were peaceful, but the cops attacked them with police dogs and fire hoses. Then there was the march on Washington and Reverend King's speech." Daniel quoted parts of it, lines beginning with *I have a dream*. It was like poetry.

"TJ was right," Daniel said. "Things have to change. You can't say people are good enough to give their lives for this country but not good enough to drink from the same water fountain as white people or eat a meal at the same lunch counter. I wish I could go down to Mississippi. TJ believed in fighting for what's right. So do I. But Ma would skin me alive."

We parted company. As I rode back to town, I kept my eyes open for a phone booth. I had to ask the operator for the number I wanted, and the next thing I knew I was talking to the woman at the front desk of the John H. Chisholm Home for the Aged.

"I came to see my grandpa yesterday. Mr. Lorne Beale?"

"Oh yes," she said. "I remember."

"But I forgot to ask…my mom wanted to know if she owes anything for Grandpa's room and board."

"Oh my, no," the woman said. "Everything is covered. You can tell your mother she doesn't have to worry about a thing."

"But she said the place is expensive, and on Grandpa's social security..."

"It's taken care of, honey. You tell your mother that your grandfather is well looked after. If she wants more information, she can write to the director."

Chapter Fourteen

I AM FOLLOWED BY AN ANGRY MOB

DANIEL WAS WAITING for me on Maggie's porch the next morning. I could see from his face that he was bursting to tell me something.

"Ma says she remembers the man who used to play piano at the roadhouse. She says he's got a place up on the river. You want to go and talk to him?"

Did I? You bet. But first I'd promised to wash some upstairs windows.

"I'll help you," Daniel said. "Twice the number of hands, half the amount of work."

I laughed. "You sound like Mrs. Hazelton."

"No. I sound like Ma."

Maggie had no objection to the extra help. I didn't think she would. When Daniel and I finished, she called us into the kitchen for sandwiches and lemonade. Daniel dug in. We ate and cleared the table, then set off on foot to the river. We followed it until we reached a small shack.

In the distance, we saw a man sitting on a fallen tree on the riverbank. He was fishing.

"Is that him?" I asked.

"I don't know. I've never met him."

Daniel called out, "Mr. Rollins?"

The fisherman turned and waited for us to approach. Daniel made the introductions and then looked at me to explain why we were there.

"Who told you where to find me?" Mr. Rollins asked.

"Daniel's mother. Mrs. Jefferson."

"*Lila* Jefferson?"

Daniel and I nodded in unison.

Mr. Rollins threw back his head and laughed. Wrinkles were etched into his face, but his teeth were pearly white, and his hair thick and black.

"Every time I ran into that woman, she'd tell me I was the devil playing the devil's music and threaten that if I didn't get myself back to church good and regular, I'd end up playing for the devil himself one day. And she told you where to find me?"

"Do you remember seeing Thomas Jefferson at the roadhouse?" I asked.

"Sure do. He used to come in regular. Had an army buddy, a white fellow from up in Canada."

"Did they have any trouble?"

"Trouble?" Mr. Rollins looked confounded. "TJ? Hell no." Embarrassment flitted across his face. "Excuse my language."

"It's okay. I won't tell Ma." Daniel smiled shyly at the old man.

"To everybody down at the Rooster—"

"The Rooster?"

"That was the name of the place. Well, actually, it was called Cock of the Walk. Owned by a fella named Abel Cain. Swear to God, that was his name. At least, he claimed it was. Everyone called his place the Rooster. And let me tell you, the joint was jumpin' back then, seven days a week. That was one of the things that put the city fathers against the place. But there was nothing they could do, because it was just across the county line. Everybody made their way down there sooner or later." He turned to Daniel. "Even your ma, although when she came down there, it was usually to drag TJ home. 'Course, that was before he came back a war hero." He laughed at the memory. "TJ started coming down there when he was younger than you. Cain wouldn't let him in. He wouldn't let any kids in. He wasn't about to close down his place of business on a Sunday, but he sure as hell didn't want any trouble from the ladies of the church for corrupting children before their time. Your brother would sit outside the window—I could see him sometimes from my piano bench. He always had a dreamy look on his face when he listened to the music. I used to think maybe he wanted to be a musician."

"TJ?" This was obviously news to Daniel.

"He played some," Mr. Rollins says.

"Played what?"

"Piano. He used to come down sometimes in the afternoon, and I'd give him a lesson. But I guess your ma didn't know about that either. He must have practiced some, because when he got back from the war, he'd come in and try to sweet-talk me into sliding off the bench so he could sit in. Usually he had to buy me a few drinks to seal the deal. And I got to hand it to the boy—he was good. Not as good as me, of course. But good all the same. All the girls used to think so, and that's a fact."

I jumped on that. "Did that cause any problems?"

"How do you mean?"

"Was someone else's girl interested in Mr. Jefferson?"

"You mean was someone jealous because his girl was mooning around the piano while TJ played? I wouldn't doubt it. He was a good-looking kid, just like his baby brother here. Had a smile that would charm the knickers off any girl. That's what his friend used to say. *And* he was a war hero. Yeah, there was probably more than one fella that wished TJ had stayed over there in Europe. But he didn't, did he?"

"Was there anyone in particular that you remember might have had a problem with him?" I asked.

"There were a few fights. Especially when folks had been drinking. But they always ended fast, usually with TJ asking the fellow involved if he really wanted to take a chance on a trained soldier. TJ was big and strong. Whatever fella it was who got himself all hot around the collar usually backed down, especially when TJ bought him a drink and sent his woman back to him."

"He didn't have his eye on anyone in particular?"

Mr. Rollins shook his head.

"TJ wasn't like that," he said. "He wasn't the kind to steal someone else's woman."

"Did he date anyone?"

"TJ?" He thought for a moment. "Not that I know of. I don't think he was settled in enough to think about that. Mostly he talked about starting a business. He wanted to make something of himself. He didn't want to have to scratch for a living. If you want my opinion, he was a first-things-first kind of fella. First he'd get himself set up, then he'd start thinking about a wife and family."

Another strikeout. I decided to try a different angle.

"Do you think he killed his friend?"

I sensed Daniel tensing up beside me.

"You mean that fella from Canada?" Mr. Rollins didn't hesitate. "No, I do not. Oh, I know what they said. I know what the jury decided. But I never believed it. For one thing, those two was good friends. And the Canadian, he was easygoing. Friendly to everyone in the place, not just the white folks."

Edgar had mentioned white kids in the Rooster too, and it had surprised me. My impression of Orrenstown was that black and white didn't mix.

"Why did the white kids go there?" I asked.

"For the music, of course," Mr. Rollins said. "It wasn't all the white kids, just the ones who didn't see much excitement in Frank Sinatra and Bing Crosby. Who wanted something livelier. Who wanted to dance. Especially the girls. They used to come down here all dressed up and looking older than they really were. My, my, how they loved to dance. I don't know what their mamas and papas would have said if they'd seen those churchgoing girls boogieing the night away."

Boogieing? Was that some kind of dance?

"I heard that the Rooster burned down in 1949," I said.

"Burned to the ground. Fire marshal said it was arson, but the police never did find out who did it—and that's assuming they even tried. That Sheriff Beale, he wasn't too interested in crimes against colored folk. But my, my, he sure was quick to make an appearance as soon as any white person made a complaint against a colored. He's the kind of sheriff they had back in the day—you tell him some colored boy made a pass at his girl or his wife, and the next thing you know, that boy is doing time and can consider himself lucky if a lynch mob doesn't show up outside the jailhouse, clamoring to string him up."

I couldn't help wondering if that's why Sheriff Beale was living beyond his obvious means at the John H. Chisholm Home for the Aged—as payment for services rendered.

"It didn't help that they found that fella in the river not half a mile from TJ's mama's house," Mr. Rollins said. "Sheriff Beale was at TJ's door as quick as a rabbit, wanting to take him in for questioning. Had to go to the Rooster to find him, and then had to back off because just about every man in the place put hisself between TJ and the sheriff, like they was daring the sheriff to arrest him."

"Really?" Daniel's eyes were wide. Clearly, he'd never heard this story before.

"Really," Mr. Rollins said. "Like I said, your brother was a hero to the colored around here, if not to the whites. People admired him. They respected him. The sheriff had to scuttle back to his car and put out a call for reinforcements. Called in his two deputies, plus the sheriff and deputies from the next county over. Sat right outside in his car until they showed up, all of them with their shotguns out and racked, ready to start firing if they had to. That was the only way they could take TJ in."

"Did he say anything?" I asked.

"TJ? Not a word. He was too smart to start mouthing off to a dozen armed police officers, all of them with twitchy trigger fingers on account of being outnumbered."

"Did he say anything about Patrice?"

"When the cops were there?" Mr. Rollins gave his head a firm shake. "When he come in earlier that night, though, he asked about him. Patrice, you say his name was? Yeah, that sounds right. TJ was asking if anyone had seen him. Said he'd been looking for him all day because they were supposed to meet with the fella that owned the garage they were wanting to buy."

"And?" I asked. "Had anyone seen him?"

"Not that day. I'm pretty sure he didn't find anyone who had seen him. I remember he looked upset."

"Upset?"

"Worried."

Why would he be worried if he already knew where Patrice was, if he'd already killed him? That didn't make sense. Unless he was worried that he'd be found out.

"Are you sure it was worry?" I asked.

"Sure as sunshine on a summer day. He was worried about what might have happened to his buddy. Guess he had good instincts, because it couldn't have been more than a day later that they found the body in the river."

"What about Patrice? Did he make any enemies?"

"Not that I know of. But then, I can't say I paid all that much attention to him. And he wasn't around nearly as much as TJ was."

"I thought you said Patrice and TJ came down to the Rooster regularly, and that Patrice was friendly to everyone."

"I said TJ came regular. Patrice came from time to time, and he was friendly when he was there. Talked to everyone. Seemed genuinely interested in what people were up to. But he wasn't there nearly as often as TJ was."

"Where was he when he wasn't there?"

Mr. Rollins laughed. "What do I look like to you? One of those women with the headdress and the big glass ball? I have no idea where he was. Probably minding his own business somewhere."

Or making enemies, I thought. It was possible. People in town didn't like that TJ strutted around, as they put it, as if he was better than everyone else. They probably didn't like it either that his buddy and soon-to-be business partner was white. I remembered the story the old men had told me.

By the time we thanked Mr. Rollins, I was already planning my next move. People in town clearly remembered Thomas Jefferson, murderer. Maybe a few of them remembered the victim.

"Now what?" Daniel said. He'd been kicking a stone in front of him all the way down the dirt road that led from the river to his house.

"How long was Patrice here before he ended up in the river?"

Daniel shrugged and kicked the stone hard. It skittered ten feet into the air, hit a larger rock and flew off into the scrub beside the road. When he got to the bigger rock, he kicked that instead.

"A week? A month? Longer?" I asked.

"TJ brought me a birthday present." His voice was so soft, so faraway, that it sounded as though he was talking to himself. "Toys from Germany. Really nice ones—a truck and a bus and some cars. All hand-painted. He said he found them in a bombed-out factory. They went inside, and there were toys everywhere. He and some of his buddies found a couple of boxes that were in perfect condition, so they threw them into the Jeep and brought them home. I still have them."

I couldn't even imagine what it was like to have something like that, a special gift from a family member, something that would forever and always remind you of that person.

"Ma told me he gave them to me three days after he got back—on my birthday. That was the beginning of April. Patrice died at the end of May."

"So TJ and Patrice were back here almost two months before Patrice died." Less than sixty days, but from what I had seen so far, a long time in a town like this, where every newcomer was noticed and speculated about. "Somebody must have gotten to know him or at least had some idea of how he spent his time when he wasn't with your brother."

"I guess." Daniel didn't sound convinced.

We walked in silence for a few minutes. Then I couldn't help it—I had to ask.

"What happened to TJ's father?"

Daniel looked at me.

"When your mom said he died, you acted kind of strange."

"That's because he didn't just die. He was lynched."

I stared at him.

"Lynched?"

"Somebody said he made a pass at a white woman, tried to assault her. He was arrested. A mob showed up at the jail and dragged him out and hung him."

I couldn't believe what I was hearing.

"Where was the sheriff?"

"I don't know anything except that's what happened, and I only know it because I heard my ma talking to one of her aunties about it after my dad died in an accident at the cannery. He got caught in some equipment and died before anyone could turn it off."

"I'm sorry."

"Ma cried for days. First she lost TJ's dad, then TJ, then my dad."

"Did anyone go to jail for what happened to TJ's dad?"

"I dunno. I doubt it."

"Didn't your ma—"

"She would never talk about it, not even when I asked her. I went to the newspaper office one time, when the old man still worked there." I guessed he meant Maggie's father. "I wanted to see what was in the newspaper about it, but there wasn't anything."

"The paper didn't cover it?"

"Some papers were missing. The old guy said they must have sold out or something. He said he didn't recall what I was talking about, but you know what? I didn't believe him."

"When...when did it happen?"

"When TJ was still a kid. That's all I know. But it's like it never happened at all. No one talks about it."

I didn't know what to say.

I stood on a sidewalk in Orrenstown and looked up and down the street. I had a plan, but I was nervous. What if people didn't want to talk to me? Sheriff Hicks had told

Maggie that I'd been seen in Freemount. People were talking about me. Maybe they'd seen me with Daniel. Maybe some people didn't like that any more than they'd liked seeing Mr. Jefferson and Mr. LaSalle together. Suddenly I felt like the old Cady, the poor little orphan girl from the Home, looked down upon by the likes of Mrs. Danforth, viewed as an unfortunate, the unwanted child of a foolish, unmarried mother, a person without a real name, without parentage, without my own "people." A girl who would never be able to lay claim to a boy like Johnny Danforth, even though he was happy to kiss and cuddle me in the woods at the edge of town. A girl Mrs. Danforth had declared, to my face, to be beneath the likes of a boy like her Johnny. A nonentity.

And then I thought about Nellie Bly.

She wasn't an orphan, but she was an outsider, at least at the beginning. She'd had to prove herself. She'd had to fight her way into a man's world, the world of her dreams, the world of a newspaper reporter. And, like Maggie, she had made it. She had broken free of the women's pages long before Maggie and other women had ever thought of doing something so daring. And she had done it by taking risks. By being bold.

If she could do it, so could I. At least, I hoped so.

I squared my shoulders and headed for the place that had so far proved to be my best source of information: the diner.

The only people there were the waitress and two older women in hats, eating tiny sandwiches and drinking tea. I ordered lemonade and, in a low voice, asked the waitress if the women were longtime residents of Orrenstown.

"Those two?" The waitress sniffed. "That one's husband manages the cannery." She nodded to the woman in the green pillbox hat. "The other one's husband owns the real-estate office. They've been here since forever. They think they're special on account of their husbands. That's why they make me cut the crusts off their sandwiches. They think it's more elegant. They must have read about sandwiches like that in those magazines they're always buying that show how to decorate your house and entertain your guests."

I'd already made up my mind. I left my lemonade on the counter and approached their table.

"I'm sorry to bother you—"

"Then don't," said the woman in the green hat. She had a pointy nose and too much rouge on her cheeks. "We're having a private conversation, aren't we, Helen?"

"Now, Eileen," Helen said. She was plump, with a round face and pale blue eyes. Once upon a time, she might have been pretty. "Don't give the girl a hard time."

"Don't you know who she is?" Eileen said. "She's that girl who's been asking about the Jefferson boy—the one that got shot escaping from prison."

Helen had a twinkle in her eye when she looked up at me again.

"Is that right?"

I admitted that it was. "I was wondering—did you know Mr. Jefferson?"

"Of course not," Eileen said.

"We certainly knew who he was," Helen said.

"Everyone knew who he was. And what he was," Eileen said. "I can't say I was surprised that he ended up the way he did."

I decided to ignore Eileen and concentrate instead on her companion.

"Did you know his friend?" I asked. "The man he's supposed to have murdered?"

"His friend? The French fellow?"

"A man with no common sense at all, if you ask me." Eileen sniffed.

"I used to see him around town from time to time," Helen said. "But no, I can't say that I knew him. I don't think I ever spoke to the man."

"Do you know anyone who might have spoken to him or known him?"

Helen thought for a moment and then shook her head.

"I can't say that I do." She didn't ask why I wanted to know.

Strikeout. But they were only two people in a town full of people.

"Can you tell me which stores and businesses were here at the time of the murder?" I asked.

Helen seemed momentarily surprised by the question. Then she broke into a smile.

"You're thinking that if he was in town for any length of time, then he would have frequented some of the businesses here. Very clever. Now, let me see. The hair salon is new. That is to say, there was always one here, but Etta sold the business when the arthritis made it impossible for her to continue. But then, I doubt your Frenchman would have stopped by there. Apart from that, I'd say pretty much everything else is the same."

She wished me luck and weathered Eileen's disapproval with aplomb.

I went from store to store and was only a little nervous. Mostly I managed to ignore the disapproving looks sent my way, and I pretended I didn't hear the whispering behind my back. Some people—the ancient brother barbers at the barbershop, the real-estate agent who I guessed was the plump woman's husband, the Eileen look-alike at the florists—told me they knew who I was and were curt, if not downright rude, when they said they didn't know anything about the man who had been murdered before I was born. A few—the gum-snapping, middle-aged bottle blond at the cash register in the grocery store, the bored cigar smoker at the candy store that featured more pinball machines than treats, the straw-hatted, sweaty-faced owner of the non-air-conditioned hardware store—allowed that they did, in fact, remember Mr. LaSalle (although they all spoke of him as *the Frenchman*), but said they knew nothing about him other than he should have picked better company—in fact, he should have stayed in his own country. If he had, he might be alive today.

By lunchtime, I had canvassed one side of the main street and learned absolutely nothing of value.

I headed back to Maggie's and found her in the parlor with Arthur, discussing what needed to be done to repair the damage done by the fire. I made lunch for them and helped Arthur carry all the furniture out of the parlor. Then I packed up all the knickknacks and carried them out. One wall was badly scorched and had to be re-drywalled. The carpet had to be taken up. Fortunately, the floor underneath had sustained only superficial damage, and that wouldn't be noticeable once Maggie bought new carpet. I washed the walls and floors while Arthur measured and made notes and finally drove off in his truck to pick up supplies. By the time he returned, I had done all I could do, so I went back downtown and canvassed the rest of the businesses. My stomach was rumbling by the time I'd finished. It was too late for supper at Maggie's, so I went back to the diner. The young waitress was gone for the day and had been replaced by an older woman with scarlet lipstick and a beehive hairdo, who took my order for a ham-and-cheese sandwich and a glass of iced tea. I ate alone in one of the booths. It was nice to be by myself and have time to think. By the time I'd finished, it was dusk. I started back to Maggie's, a fifteen-minute walk.

As I crossed the street, I glimpsed myself in a store window. That's when I saw about a dozen people crossing directly behind me. They were all male, and most of them were older than me. They were all grim-faced. I paused to let them pass, but they didn't. They stopped and stared at me. It was creepy. I turned and started walking again, faster this time. I didn't look back until I had reached the bottom of Maggie's street. I didn't have to. I heard their footsteps behind me. My heart raced. They were following me. But why? I fought the urge to break into a run.

I thought about the fire at Maggie's and Sheriff Hicks's theory that it was because of me. If he was right—and I suspected he was—then I'd caused Maggie enough trouble. I turned to face the mob, telling myself that surely they wouldn't hurt me on a quiet residential street where anyone could look out a window and see what they were doing.

The men formed a tight circle around me. One of them pressed so close that I smelled the tobacco and beer on his breath. He looked at me with contempt.

"You got no business in this town. If you're here to stir up trouble like those college kids down south, then you're going to get trouble, you'd better believe it. We don't need any strangers, especially any New Yorkers, telling us what we should and shouldn't do."

"I'm not here to make trouble." I tried to sound calm and reasonable, but it was impossible to hide the tremor in my voice.

"You've been hanging around with that boy, the one whose brother was a murderer."

"I thought this was a free country," I said. "I thought people could associate with whomever they please."

The *whomever* was a mistake. When the ringleader heard it, he repeated it jeeringly.

"We got a genuine college student here, come to tell us what's what." He stepped even closer, so that our noses almost touched. I recoiled automatically—and bumped into the man directly behind me. That did it. If their mission was to scare me, they had succeeded. I looked frantically around, but there wasn't another soul on the street. And it was getting dark.

"If you know what's good for you, you'll get out of town," the ringleader said. "The sooner, the better—for you."

The men crowded closer, as if they intended to smother me with their bodies. I balled my hands into tight fists. I had no idea what they were going to do to me, but I intended to fight back.

A bright light struck the knot of men. A teenager on the outside of the group raised a hand to protect his eyes. I heard a vehicle and a familiar voice.

"What's going on there, fellas?" It was Mr. Standish—I was sure of it.

The circle grew ragged at the edges as a couple of the men stepped back.

"This is nothing for you to be concerned about, doc," the ringleader said without taking his eyes off me.

I heard a truck door open and close. Leather-soled shoes slapped the cement sidewalk. The circle parted to admit Mr. Standish.

"I see." He shook his head and let out a heavy sigh. "Come on, young lady. I'll give you a lift home." He sounded like a weary father who had just found his naughty offspring doing something she shouldn't be—again. He turned and came face-to-face with a wall of men. He didn't say a word but looked at each man in turn. A couple of them bowed their heads as if they were ashamed and shuffled out of his way.

I had to shoulder my way past the ringleader, who scowled at me. No one else gave me trouble. I followed Mr. Standish to his tired old pickup truck. Most of the group trailed after us, but Mr. Standish didn't hurry or betray any nervousness. He circled around to the passenger-side door and opened it for me. He drove me up the street to Maggie's and pulled over to the curb.

"You want to watch those boys," he said. "They may act like idiots, but they're dangerous idiots. You understand what I mean?"

I said I did, and I wondered where he situated himself. Was he with the mob or against it? Were his words a warning for me to get out of town, or was he genuinely concerned that something might happen? I couldn't tell.

"I heard you were out at the old folks' home," he said. "Heard you were pretending to be Lorne Beale's granddaughter."

"That's not true." I was grateful that he'd rescued me but furious at his question. How did he know where I'd been? Had he followed me? Was there some kind of spy network in this town?

"I know people who work out there." Mr. Standish turned in his seat to look at me. "You were there, all right."

"But I never said I was his granddaughter."

"I knew it was you the minute I heard a girl went to see him. That granddaughter of his wouldn't come within a hundred miles of here, not after what her mother told her. Jane—that's the mother's name—made it known when she left here that she wanted nothing to do with the old man. The house in town, his cabin—she said to sell them and burn the money, for all she cared."

That piqued my interest. "Because of what happened to Mr. Jefferson?"

"Because of what happened long before that. Lorne and his daughter never saw eye to eye. I think Jane must have poisoned the girl against him. Then, if you ask me, Lorne made a mistake letting the girl go to a fancy boarding school up north after her mother died. She became a different person entirely. She butted heads with Lorne every time she came home, until pretty soon she stopped coming altogether. She didn't invite him to her wedding. Didn't even tell him she was getting married. He heard about it from one of his wife's old aunties."

"I never said I was his granddaughter. People just assumed."

"And you let them." But there was no reproach in his voice. "What are you doing here, Cady?"

"Minding my own business." I reached for the door handle.

"You best be careful."

I jumped down from the truck. Maggie was sitting outside reading. She looked up when the truck stopped at the curb and frowned when I stepped under the porch light.

"You're so pale. And goodness, you're shaking. Are you all right?" She looked at the truck driving away. "That was Miles Standish, wasn't it? What's going on, Cady?"

I told her.

Maggie sank back into her chair.

"You have to be careful, Cady. People around here have some pretty set ideas. It's going to take a lot to change the way they see things."

"But I'm not hurting anyone. I just want to find out why everything about Mr. Jefferson's trial is missing."

"That may seem like nothing to you. But there's a reason I left this town, apart from it being too small and offering girls no opportunities other than matrimony. People here think and do exactly what their parents and grandparents thought and did. They're comfortable with things the way they are, and they're not comfortable with anyone trying to make changes."

"That's not what I'm doing."

"I know that, and you know that. But those men who followed you don't know that. All they know is that a bunch of what they would call *foreign agitators* have gone down to Mississippi, where they're trying to change the way things have always been. They don't even like it when Washington tells them they have to let black kids go to the same schools as white kids or that black people can sit anywhere they want on a bus. You already know what they thought of Thomas Jefferson when he came back from the war and objected to being treated like a second-class citizen."

"But—"

"There was a time not so long ago when the Ku Klux Klan was active here."

I'd been wondering about that ever since I looked at the newspaper clipping Mrs. Hazelton had given me. I knew a little about the KKK, but I'd always thought of it as a southern phenomenon. Maggie set me straight.

"Back when I was born, there were probably three or four million Klan members across the country. They had 250,000 members right here in Indiana. They say that one in three white males in this state were members. In some towns, you couldn't get elected to public office without Klan support."

I was stunned to hear this.

"Just because there are no segregated drinking fountains here doesn't mean that everyone treats everyone else equally. That day will come, God willing, but it isn't here yet. And right now people are nervous about what's going on in Mississippi and Alabama. They think if one race gets something, then the other loses. That's not true, of course. But that's the way people think." She studied me in the light from overhead. "I know you think this Thomas Jefferson thing is important, and maybe to you it is. Maybe it will turn out to be important for this town. But you have to tread softly, Cady. People aren't going to change overnight just because you think they should. Change takes time."

I didn't have time. I couldn't stay down here forever. And I didn't intend to go back to Toronto without a story, one with a beginning, a middle and an end.

Chapter Fifteen

I VISIT THE SCENE OF THE CRIME

I DID HOUSEWORK all morning and then told Maggie I had to run a few errands. It was a lie, but I didn't want her to worry about me. She didn't ask where I was going. All she said was, "Be careful."

I met up with Daniel, and he led me to where Patrice's body had been found. It was downstream from some rapids formed by a narrowing of the river.

I stared into the roiling water. What wasn't foam was the color of milk chocolate.

"Has the water always been so muddy?" I asked.

"Far as I know."

A length of tree branch swirled past us, moved quickly through the rapids and vanished.

"If you dumped a body here, wouldn't the current carry it away?"

"If you mean Patrice's body, it wasn't just dumped. It was weighted down. I told you that. The killer chose that place because the water is so deep, and because of the rapids people don't come here very often."

"If the body was weighted down, then how was it found? I can't see anything in there. And if people don't come here often, why would anyone think to look for it here?"

"There was a big storm just before they found him. Everyone says if it wasn't for that storm, he might never have been found."

"What do you mean?"

"His body was tied to an old metal pulley, a really big one. But the rope broke during the storm, and he floated to the surface."

I shuddered at the thought.

"The body floated to the surface," Mr. Standish said. I'd found him in the first place I looked: the diner, talking over coffee with Mr. Selig and Mr. Drew. He waved me into a chair—clearly, there were no hard feelings from the night before—and ordered me a cup of coffee.

"Way I heard it, the rope didn't hold," Mr. Drew said. "Seems to me they didn't teach those boys proper knot tying while they were in the army."

"Knots are for the navy," Mr. Standish said mildly.

"Bad luck though," Mr. Selig said. "If he'd tied the rope good and proper, he might have got away with it. It wasn't like anyone was going to check where that fella had gone.

If anyone gave him a second thought, they'd think he finally smartened up and got himself back where he belonged." He sipped his coffee. "Yes sir, if I was that boy, I surely would have checked that knot."

I had another question.

"Was someone looking for Mr. LaSalle? Or did someone just find him accidentally?"

Mr. Standish frowned thoughtfully. Mr. Selig shook his head. Mr. Drew said, "The Jefferson boy was looking for him. He came by the store and asked if he'd been around."

"Marcus owned a feed and seed store back then," Mr. Standish explained. "His nephew runs it now. That one and two more. A regular chain."

"A short chain." Mr. Drew laughed.

"So only Mr. Jefferson was looking for Mr. LaSalle?" I asked. "Nobody else?"

"Can't think why anyone else would," Mr. Selig said. "He was a stranger in town. The only thing we knew about him was that he was Jefferson's friend."

"And a Frenchie," Mr. Drew said.

"And a soldier," Mr. Standish said.

"All adds up to a whole lot of not much," Mr. Selig said stubbornly. "Why would anyone look for a stranger?"

But I couldn't help thinking, Why would Mr. Jefferson have looked for Mr. LaSalle? If he really had killed him, tied his body to a pulley and dumped it in the deepest, muddiest part of the river he could find, why would he go around town looking for him? Wouldn't that just call attention to the fact that Mr. LaSalle was missing? Why didn't he keep his mouth shut and if the subject came up (unlikely, according to these three old men), tell whoever asked that LaSalle had gone back home? Nobody would have questioned that.

"Who found the body?" I asked.

"Sheriff Hicks. Of course, he was just Deputy Hicks back then. I guess he would have been on the job for about two years at the time."

It was after dark, and I was in the kitchen waxing the floor—it needed it—when I heard a *swoosh*. A large manila envelope slid under the kitchen door and halfway across the floor. Printed on the front were the words *For the girl staying at Maggie's.* I pushed open the kitchen door and stepped out into the heavy night air in time to see someone—a black woman—hurrying down Maggie's driveway. I called out, but she didn't stop.

I went back into the kitchen and opened the envelope. Inside was a file folder. I slipped it out and opened it. It contained three black-and white-photographs. The first made me flinch. It was an eight-by-ten police photograph of a body, badly bloated, its hands and ankles bound. Something was wound around its waist. I stared at it. There was a river in the background. It looked like the same place Daniel took me to—the place where Patrice LaSalle's body was found. I shuffled the photo to the bottom and looked at the next one.

It was a close-up of...of what, exactly? It looked like a piece of heavy equipment—like a giant pulley. Which was exactly what it was. It was the pulley Daniel had told me about, the one that had been used to weight Mr. LaSalle's body and keep it hidden beneath the surface of the muddy water. I moved to the next picture.

The third and last photograph showed the body with the pulley beside it. Where had these pictures come from? Who was the woman who had delivered them? And why had she left them for me? To scare me? To warn me of what might happen to me if I continued to ask questions about Mr. Jefferson and Mr. LaSalle? Did that group of men put her up to delivering them?

I was slipping the photos back into the envelope when something caught my eye. I stepped directly under the overhead light and studied the third photo again. I flipped back to the second one. Was I really seeing what I thought I was seeing? If I was, what did it mean?

In the first picture, the body's hands and feet were bound with rope. It was as plain as day. But the binding around the waist—that wasn't rope. It was some kind of wire, but it was thick, like cable.

I flipped to the second picture, and then the third. There was no doubt about it. One end of the cable was attached to the body, the other end to the pulley. But the cable wasn't in one piece. It looked as though it had been cut.

I sat down at the table, spread the three photos out in front of me and tried to estimate how much cable there was altogether. It didn't look very long. Maybe three or four feet.

Daniel had said the river was deep where the body was found. But how deep was deep? Surely more than three feet. At three feet, a man could stand up and the water would hit the top of his thighs, or maybe his waist if he was short. The river had to be a lot deeper than that. So if the body had been attached to the pulley by cable, and if the pulley was at the bottom of the river, then there was no way the body would ever have bobbed to the surface.

One of the old men—was it Mr. Selig or Mr. Drew?—had said that if Mr. Jefferson had been better at tying knots, the body would never have been found. But you tie a knot in a rope, not in a cable. And besides, this was a crime-scene photo, I was sure of it, and the cable was still wrapped around both the body and the pulley. There was no knot. Yet somehow the cable had ended up in two pieces. There was only one way that could have happened: someone must have cut it. But when? And why? Why cut the cable and leave the body floating in the river where someone might find it? That was the question that ate at me all night.

I was up and out of Maggie's house at sunrise the next morning. I planted myself on a bench across the street from the sheriff's office and watched until I saw a familiar figure get out of a car.

"Sheriff Hicks!" I ran across the street.

The sheriff, his uniform shirt crisp at the beginning of what promised to be a hot day, the crease in his pants knife-sharp, squinted into the rising sun at me.

"Cady. You still in town?"

"I need to ask you a question."

I saw a flicker of impatience in his eyes. "Shoot," he said.

"It's about the man that Mr. Jefferson killed."

"What about him?"

"I heard you were the one who found the body."

There was a tick of hesitation before he answered, and I couldn't help thinking that he was wondering how I knew that. He nodded.

"Where did you find it?"

"In the river."

"In a deep part of it, where the rapids are, right?"

"I don't recall exactly. It was a long time ago."

"Someone showed me the spot."

"Well, that person has a better memory than I do," he said. "I'd have to look it up."

"Okay." I looked expectantly at him.

"But I'm not going to do that," he said. "In the first place, like I told you, the records from that time were destroyed in the flood. And in the second place, I have a lot of work to do. I don't have time to worry over cases that were closed before you were even born." He locked his car and started for the stairs.

"Can I ask you one more question?"

"Would it make any difference if I said no?"

"How did you find the body?"

"What do you mean?"

"How did you find it? Were you out looking for Mr. LaSalle?"

"I don't recall that anyone was looking for him. He'd supposedly left town."

"Who told you that?"

"I believe it was Jefferson."

"That can't be right," I said. "Mr. Jefferson was looking for him. He was asking people around town if they'd seen him."

"Now how would you know that?"

"I asked around."

"Did you, now?" The sheriff shook his head. "Why do I get the idea that there's more to you than meets the eye? You're sticking to this thing like a puppy to a root. What's it to you?"

I dodged the question.

"Are you sure Mr. Jefferson said that Mr. LaSalle left town?" I asked.

"That's my recollection, but I guess I could be mistaken. I was just a deputy at the time. Sheriff Beale handled the case."

"But you found the body."

"I did."

"So you just happened to be passing that part of the river and you saw it?"

"Something like that."

I thought about the river and the rutted dirt road that ran alongside it.

"Were you on your way somewhere?"

"Must have been."

"Where?"

Sheriff Hicks made a show of consulting his wristwatch. "I have work to do."

"What about the cable?" I asked.

"What cable?"

"The body was anchored with a cable and a pulley so that it would stay under water, isn't that right?"

He didn't answer.

"Did you cut the cable after you pulled him up, or had the cable already been cut?" I asked.

"I don't recall."

"Because a lot of people I talked to seem to think the body was tied to that pulley with a rope."

"These would be the same people who told you where the body was found?"

I saw no harm in letting him think this.

"Like I said, the people you're talking to seem to have better memories than me," he said.

"You don't remember if it was a cable or a rope?"

"It was a long time ago."

"If I'd seen something like that, I'm sure I'd never forget."

"Well, you're not a police officer." The sheriff consulted his watch again. "Now, if you'll excuse me." He tipped his hat and strode away.

Chapter Sixteen

I AM GIVEN ANOTHER PHOTOGRAPH

I NEEDED TO think. Walking is best for that. Mindless chores that keep my hands occupied and my brain free to wander are second best. So when Maggie said that she wished she had time to pick the strawberries that grew wild at the back of her property, I volunteered. I grabbed a bucket, headed beyond the ornamental hedge that divided the lawn from the kitchen garden—Maggie grew all kinds of vegetables and herbs—and set to work. While I picked, I thought about everything I knew. I had filled two containers by the time Daniel's head appeared above the hedge. He waved something at me. I straightened immediately.

"What have you got there?" I asked.

"Mr. Rollins gave it to me." He came through the hedge and handed it to me. *It* was a framed photograph—an old one. The glass was cracked and the frame was chipped.

"It's the Rooster." I knew it immediately, even though there was no signage to confirm it. Mr. Rollins, younger but still recognizable, was seated at a piano, his head back, his face split by a wide grin. He was clearly enjoying himself. So were the people around him.

"That's TJ." Daniel pointed to a young black man standing near the piano.

"He's really handsome." He was tall and well built, with twinkling eyes.

"And that—" He pointed to a blond girl in a tight sweater and a full skirt that fell to mid-calf. She was wearing saddle shoes and ankle socks. "That's Anne Morrison. She was Anne Tyson then."

"You know her?"

He shook his head. "Mr. Rollins found the picture after we talked to him. He told me that girl used to come to the Rooster with her friends. Maybe she remembers Mr. LaSalle."

I took another look at the photo. There were at least a dozen white kids in it, half of them girls.

"How come he remembers her?"

Daniel smiled.

"He says she was a good dancer. Really good. He says he's pretty sure her mother would have packed her off to a convent school if she'd seen how that girl danced."

She certainly had a wide grin on her face. And she was pretty.

"Do you know where she is now?"

"Mr. Rollins says she still lives in town."

"Then she must be in the phone book." I looked at the strawberries. Maggie wanted to make jam. She would need more berries than I had picked so far. "Come and help me. Then we'll see if we can track down Anne."

It took us just thirty minutes to fill every container I could find with plump, fragrant strawberries. Warm from the sun, they already smelled like the strawberry jam they were destined to become.

I started back to the house, but Daniel didn't follow.

"Aren't you coming?" I asked.

He shook his head. "I'll wait here."

I delivered the strawberries and thumbed through the phone book. It contained seven Morrisons, and I couldn't help wondering if they were related to each other. I copied down all the addresses and took them out to Daniel, who was waiting at the hedge.

"Which one do you think might be her?" I showed him the list of addresses.

"This one is out of town a ways." He pointed to the first name. "This one too. The other five are closer."

I wished he could have narrowed it down even more. But five names were better than seven.

"Which is the closest one?"

He pointed.

"Show me."

He hesitated but finally walked me down to the main street. Three men stood in front of the hardware store. One of them turned and looked at us as we passed on the other side of the street. I was positive that he had followed me home with the mob the other night. He nudged his buddies, and they turned to look too. I prayed they wouldn't follow us and make trouble.

They stayed where they were. I breathed a sigh of relief.

Daniel came to a halt at an intersection.

"Go up to the first corner. That's Mulberry. The first Morrison lives there."

"You aren't coming with me?"

"I'd rather wait over there." He nodded to a bench across the street, in front of a small park.

I didn't argue with him. I sort of knew how he felt. I'd always felt out of place when I ventured into Johnny's neighborhood, where all the houses had neat lawns and shiny cars in the garage and toys strewn all over the driveway. Going there reminded me of all the things I didn't have, like parents and siblings and a house and a room of my very own—things Johnny took for granted.

"I'll be back as soon as I can," I said.

The Mrs. Morrison who answered my knock at the first house was eighty if she was a day. She peered at me through glasses that were a quarter of an inch thick, and I had to practically shout so that she would hear me. Even then, I had to repeat everything, sometimes more than once. It turned out that the Anne Morrison I was looking for was her granddaughter-in-law and the fourth of the five in-town Morrisons on my list. I shouted my thanks and went to find Daniel.

He gave me directions to Anne Morrison's house but refused to go with me. I promised to tell him what, if anything, I found out.

Anne Morrison was still a blond with salon-coiffed hair, but she was chubbier than in the photograph, and there were fine lines radiating out around her eyes and her mouth, which were made up with blue eye shadow and pink lipstick. She was wearing a cotton dress and white sandals; little pearl earrings dangled from her earlobes. She blinked at me when she opened the door and said, "Yes?" in a soft voice.

"Are you the Anne Morrison who used to be Anne Tyler?" I asked.

A frown deepened the lines on her forehead.

"Why do you ask?"

I showed her the photograph.

"Is this you?" I pointed to the slender blond.

At first Anne's eyes stayed on me. She was probably wondering who this stranger at her door was. But eventually her gaze slipped down to the framed photo, and a smile transformed her face. In an instant, she looked like the exuberant girl she used to be.

"Where on earth did you get that?" She reached for the frame, then paused and said, "May I?" When I handed her the picture, she held it up for closer inspection. "Good heavens, I didn't even know this existed."

"Mr. Rollins had it."

Anne's expression was vague. She couldn't make the connection.

"The man who used to play piano at the Rooster," I said.

"Rolly?" She squealed like a schoolgirl. "Rolly had this?"

"He says you used to sneak down to the Rooster all the time."

"So did this boy here." Anne pointed to a lanky youth, his hair slicked back, black-framed glasses all but obscuring his eyes. "That's Ronald. My husband. We met at the Rooster, although, believe me, we never told our parents. They would have had a fit if—" She broke off. Her smile faded. She fixed me with a sharp look. "I'm sorry, but who did you say you were?"

I told her that I was staying with Maggie. "The publisher of the local newspaper," I added. If she inferred from what I said that I was a relative of Maggie's or a houseguest, well, I didn't disabuse her of the notion.

"I never get a chance to look at the newspaper," she said. "The kids run me off my feet. I don't have time to sit down for even a moment. I'd be chasing them around the property right now if Ronald's mother hadn't scooped them up an hour ago to take them to a movie. There's a new Disney picture playing." She raised the photo again and smiled at some secret memory.

"I was wondering," I said. "Do you remember a man who used to go to the Rooster about the same time as you did? He was a friend of Thomas Jefferson's." I pointed him out to her.

"I didn't really know any of those boys very well."

"The man I mean was white. His name was Patrice LaSalle."

Anne's forehead scrunched up as she thought. "I don't recall—" Her eyes popped. "Say, you don't mean the man who was murdered? His name was Patrick, I think."

"Patrice."

"He had some kind of accent. He wasn't from around here. I think he was from up north somewhere."

"Canada," I said.

"That sounds right. A good-looking fellow. Dark eyes, dark hair. A soft way of speaking. Never danced. I know. I must have asked him a dozen times. Didn't talk much either. But he sure seemed to enjoy the music. His toe was always tapping."

My heart raced. This woman remembered him. She'd noticed things about him that no one else had mentioned so far.

"I tell you, even though I was sweet on Ronald—we were pinned—there were times when I couldn't take my eyes off that fellow. There was something about him. I can't say exactly what it was, but there was something. All the girls tried to get him to dance. He'd just smile and shake his head and say he was too old for that sort of thing. And we all left it at that. We were sixteen, maybe seventeen."

She smiled again. "Ronald got us some phony IDs. That way the owner could pretend he thought we were legitimate." The memory seemed to tickle her. "We were pretty wild back then. That friend of the Jefferson boy was, let me see, my God, he must have been twenty-three or twenty-four. An old man. At least, that's what we thought at the time. Wouldn't I love to be that age again!" She laughed.

"Do you remember seeing him outside of the Rooster? Do you have any idea if he made any friends here?"

"I don't know much about him except that he was found in the river. They put that Jefferson boy in prison for it."

I waited.

"We were all shocked," she said. "Some girls cried when they heard, even though they didn't know him very well. Just the idea that anyone could kill such a nice man—it seemed so awful. One of the girls, Ellie, had a breakdown over it. At least, that's what people said."

This was news. "A breakdown over the murder?"

"She was the worst for flirting with him. But he turned her down every time. After a while she stopped coming around." She thought for a moment. "Hmmm," she said.

"Hmmm?"

"I was just thinking—never mind. It's not important."

"I'm trying to get as much information as I can."

Anne looked at me. "It's just...Ellie stopped coming down to the Rooster. After that, it seemed like he wasn't there as often either. It's probably a coincidence. I mean, it's not like I ever saw them together. But it's kind of strange, now that I think of it." She shrugged.

"Did you ever talk to Ellie about it?"

"No. She left town after it happened. The murder, I mean. I didn't see her again for, I don't know, it must have been a year. I ran into her on the street. She looked thin, that's all I remember. We were never close friends, and she didn't seem to recognize me, so..." Both shoulders rose in apology. "I never spoke to her again."

"Is she still in town?" If Ellie had known Patrice LaSalle, I definitely wanted to talk to her.

"In a manner of speaking. She died. Years ago. She's buried in Oak Grove."

My spirits crashed. Another dead end. Now what?

"Was there anyone else who seemed especially interested in Mr. LaSalle?" I asked.

"Not that I recall." Anne handed the photograph back to me. "I have a million things to do now that my little monsters are out with their grandma."

"This girl Ellie," I said before she closed the door on me. "Does she have family in town?"

"Oh my, yes. Her father is John Chisholm."

"The John Chisholm who owns a lot of businesses around here?"

"The same. That's why I didn't know Ellie well. No one did. Her daddy sent her to private school up in Evansville. If you ask me, she would have been happier if he'd let her go to school with the rest of us. She would have had more friends, that's for sure."

She excused herself and disappeared inside.

I was on my way back to Maggie's when someone called my name. It was Mr. Standish. He was coming out of the drugstore.

"I was just going to get a cold drink," he said. "Care to join me?"

The man was still a mystery to me. He seemed to pop up everywhere. He knew a lot about the town and its people, and he seemed happy to share his knowledge. But there was something beneath his friendly exterior, something I couldn't quite put my finger on. Still, he was a good source of information. I accepted his invitation.

We went to the diner, where he selected a booth far from the window. Mr. Standish ordered iced tea for both of us, and while we waited for it, we made small talk. After we'd been served, though, he leaned back against the upholstered booth and said, "What are you really doing here, Cady? Why are you so interested in Thomas Jefferson?"

I met his pale eyes. In most of our encounters, Mr. Standish had been friendly, like a kindly old uncle. But I wasn't reading any uncle-like friendliness in his eyes now. There was a steely hue to the blue of his irises. Whatever he used to do before he retired, I was sure he had given it his full attention and had been successful at it. He had the air of a man of competence, someone who meant business and was businesslike in all his dealings. Someone who was used to people paying attention to him, doing what they were told and addressing him with respect.

"I already told you. I want to write about it." I sipped my iced tea demurely through a straw.

"You're stirring up trouble too, even though you told me you weren't a troublemaker."

I opened my mouth to protest, but Mr. Standish waved me to silence.

"That group of yahoos following you. The fire at Maggie's. Letting folks think you're Lorne Beale's granddaughter. It all adds up to trouble."

That reminded me of something I wanted to know.

"You told me that Sheriff Beale and his daughter didn't get along. What happened between them?"

Mr. Standish shook his head. "You're not going to let it be, are you?"

He was right about that. "What happened?"

He sighed and drank some tea.

"I told you. Lorne's wife left him, took the girl and went back to where she came from. A few years later, she died. After that, Jane—that's the daughter's name—lived with her mother's people up in Connecticut. Lorne didn't fight it. He figured she'd get a good education, which they were more than happy to pay for. She was up there all fall and winter.

I don't think she even came back for Christmas most years. But she'd make the trip most summers with a pocketbook full of money from her grandparents. She loved to party. Lorne didn't approve, but he didn't have much say in the matter. He'd more or less given that up when he agreed to let his wife's relatives foot the bills for her. There used to be a place the kids liked to hang out. A roadhouse."

The Rooster. I didn't tell him that I knew about the place. I had already learned that different people looked differently at things and remembered them differently, and if you wanted to get a good picture of what had really happened, you had to keep your mouth shut and your ears open.

"Mostly it was a colored place," Mr. Standish said. "There was music—not the kind that most parents thought was proper for their sons and daughters—and drinking. Who knows what else went on? Kids would sneak down there without their parents knowing. Well, without most parents knowing. But Lorne patrolled the place. He went in there regularly even though it was across the county line, because people around here complained about the noise and about seeing kids drive away from there at all hours. The first time he found Jane in that place, he was furious. He went in there to roust her out. Threatened to tell the other kids' parents what they were up to too. Threatened to close the place down."

He took a sip of his tea. "But that never happened."

"Because he had no authority?" I asked. "Because it was out of his jurisdiction?"

"That wasn't it. He could have done whatever he wanted and asked forgiveness afterward. He wouldn't have had trouble getting it either. No, the problem was that he hadn't bargained on Jane."

"What do you mean?"

"The story is that after Lorne threatened her, Jane took him aside for a brief conversation. Apparently, she did most of the talking. When she was finished, Lorne walked out of the place. I don't think he ever went back. I'm not even sure he kept the place on the patrol route."

"What did she say to him?"

"That *is* the question, isn't it? As far as I know, there are only two people who know the answer—Jane and Lorne. And neither one of them, to my knowledge, ever revealed the content of that particular conversation."

"What do you *think* she said?"

"My guess—she probably told him that if he ever wanted to see her again, he'd better back off and let her have her fun. She came down again the next summer, and that was it. She never came back again. Maybe Lorne went up to Connecticut to visit her. If he did, he never told me about it. And, as I already told you, she didn't invite her father to her wedding."

"Does she know he's in a nursing home?"

"I expect so. She still has a few friends down here. But she's never visited him, to my knowledge. Neither has Lorne's granddaughter. My guess is she'd be about your age. I know for a fact that Jane told Roger Whiteside—he's a lawyer, does a lot of wills and estates work—that she doesn't care what's in his will; she has no interest in anything that belongs to her father. His house was sold. Most of his stuff was either auctioned off or given away. The money's just sitting in a bank account somewhere. He's got a hunting cabin in the woods. Nice piece of lakeside property. She'll probably sell that too, if she hasn't already, and the proceeds will go into the same bank account. Roger has to keep his own counsel. But his wife overheard a conversation between Jane and Roger. Says she couldn't help overhearing it—it was more of a shouting match, really. Jane told Roger that when the time comes, she's going to give what's left of her father's estate to the NAACP. You heard of them?"

They were in the newspaper a lot. They were a civil rights organization—the National Association for the Advancement of Colored People.

"She said that would be sure to make him turn over in his grave, and she liked the idea of that." He shook his head. "No, sir. If you ask me, he never should have let Sally take that girl. It just turned her against him."

I sipped the rest of my iced tea and wondered. Finally I asked, "Did you know Ellie Chisholm?"

The question seemed to hit him like a stray ball from left field.

"You mean John Chisholm's daughter?"

I nodded.

"What about her?"

"What do you know about her?"

Mr. Standish's eyes narrowed. "You ask a lot of questions, and I have no idea where some of them come from. What do *you* know about Ellie Chisholm?"

"I know she liked to go to the same roadhouse as Jane Beale."

"So you already heard about the place."

"I know that she went to a private school too. Were she and Jane friends?"

"They probably knew each other. But they didn't go to the same school. Ellie stayed in state. What does Ellie have to do with this?"

"I don't know. Maybe nothing."

He shook his head. "Well, if you want to know anything about her, I'm afraid you'll have to ask someone else. But good luck. John Chisholm is an important man around here. He employs a lot of people. He's friendly enough, but he doesn't like to get overly familiar with people. He also likes to keep his private life to himself."

"I heard Ellie was awfully young when she died. Was she sick?"

"I heard it was an accident. I think she was away at school at the time. More than that, I don't know."

It didn't surprise me. There seemed to be a lot of secrets in this town. It reminded me of Hope. On the one hand, most people knew most other people by sight and probably also knew where they worked, if they were married or had kids, if they spent too much time at the local beer hall or the bingo, how well or poorly they dressed their kids. On the other hand, people were guarded, especially about what went on in their own homes. That was their business and no one else's. At least, that's what they strove for. No one wanted to live in a glass house. No one wanted their whole life on display for others to comment on or gossip about. People wanted to feel that they could be themselves once they closed their front doors. They wanted to be able to give in to their secret desires and longings, no matter how sad or pathetic or shameful others might judge those to be.

I finished my drink and started to slide out of the booth.

Mr. Standish laid a hand over mine to stop me.

"I think it's time for you to go back where you came from, young lady. I don't think this is a good place for you."

He was deadly serious. Was he warning me? Was he threatening me? What exactly was going on? For *sure* it had something to do with Thomas Jefferson. That's what had brought me down here. It's what had gotten me into trouble with that mob. It may have been behind the fire. I was definitely getting the message that people—some people anyway—didn't want me looking into Mr. Jefferson's past. It made me more determined to find out what was going on.

Maggie had left me a note. She was covering a council meeting in a nearby town and then had to attend a birthday party for a woman who was turning 102. She wouldn't be back until suppertime. There was no one in the house, no guests other than Arthur, and I wasn't sure about him because I hadn't seen him in two days.

I went downstairs to the morgue. This time I made a beeline for the file cabinets and looked up *Chisholm*. There were two files. One was as fat as a New York City phone book—or, at least, how I imagined a New York City phone book would look. It was a file on John Chisholm. The second was slender—*Chisholm, Ellie*. The only thing inside that one was an obituary, written out by hand. Ellie Chisholm had been nineteen when she died *suddenly*. It listed her accomplishments—head of her class all through school, member of her school basketball team, an excellent gymnast, cello player, member of her school yearbook committee, member of the debate club, editor of her school newspaper. A girl of many accomplishments. But there was no mention of how she died. No mention, even, of the accident that Mr. Standish said took her life.

Maybe that meant something, and maybe it didn't. I had nothing that tied Ellie Chisholm to Patrice LaSalle. She had flirted with him—all the girls had, according to Anne Morrison. Also according to Anne, Ellie had stopped going to the Rooster about the same time Patrice did. That could mean something, or it could mean nothing at all.

But suppose it meant something.

Suppose Ellie and Mr. LaSalle—Patrice—had stopped going to the Rooster at the same time because they wanted to be alone with each other. It was possible. But then, when you theorize without the benefit of any firm facts, almost anything is possible. The trick is finding out if it really happened. It was frustrating to think that Ellie Chisholm had known Patrice LaSalle better than most people but that it was impossible to ask her about him.

Unless...

Maybe she had confided in someone at home.

Maybe she had confided in her father.

Chapter Seventeen

I GO TO THE BIG HOUSE

IT WASN'T HARD to find out where John Chisholm lived. It was a lot harder to actually get there. And it took a lot longer than I would have wished—forty-eight minutes on Maggie's bicycle, to be exact—because Mr. Chisholm lived on a large farm outside of town. It had a red barn just like in a picture book, three silos, and a pickup in the driveway. East of the barn, separated from the barnyard by a tight row of mature poplars, was a large square, white-clapboard house with a red wraparound veranda and red gingerbread trim, its gabled windows gleaming in the afternoon sun, its lawn evenly mowed, its flower beds thick with blossoms. But the place looked deserted. The only person in sight was a man on a tractor at the far end of a field. He'd been made so small by distance that he looked like a toy man on a toy tractor. Was he Mr. Chisholm?

I climbed the verandah steps and rang the doorbell. A black woman in a cotton dress and a crisp white apron asked me for my name and my business and told me to wait. I stood on the porch and looked around until she returned to inform me that Mr. Chisholm would see me. We walked through a cool marble-floored front hall, past a massive living room with rugged, overstuffed furniture, mostly in leather, past a billiards room with a bar at one end and plenty of chairs for spectators, past what looked like a den or an office, through a sun-filled kitchen and out onto the back verandah, where a silver-haired man in khaki pants and a short-sleeved white shirt was sitting with his newspaper and a glass of what looked like lemonade. He turned expectantly when the door to the verandah opened and inspected me with unconcealed curiosity when he saw me. But, like a gentleman, he got to his feet and put a smile on his face.

"Miss Andrews, is it?" He extended his hand. "John Chisholm. Please sit and tell me what I can do for you." To the woman: "Alice, please get some lemonade for Miss Andrews. She looks parched."

A glass of frosty lemonade sounded like heaven. Even on a bike, the trip from town had been hot and dusty. The woman was back only seconds later with a glass that clinked with ice. I drank as much as I could get away with in polite company without appearing greedy. I hated to set down the glass unfinished, but Mrs. Hazelton had drilled certain ladylike practices into us. *Never start eating before the host or hostess. Take small bites. Don't slurp your soup or drink it directly from the bowl. Don't gulp your milk* (or lemonade).

The whole time, Mr. Chisholm waited patiently and watched me with a bland face. But his eyes never left me, even when he reached for the silver cigarette case, buffed to a blinding finish, sitting on the small table between us. He took out a cigarette and lit it with a tabletop silver-and-crystal lighter, the kind that people display proudly on a shelf or end table. His white shirt and crisp pants were spotless. His cream-and-tan shoes were buffed and mark-free. His hair was swept back from his forehead. His clean-shaven face was smooth and pinkish. And the house! The house stretched to either side of me and looked out over a freshly manicured lawn. At its farthest extremes were magnificent shade trees that must have been planted at least a century ago.

"It's about your daughter," I said. There was a slight tremor in my voice. His wealth and standing in the community were intimidating.

"That much I gathered from Alice," he said. "But why are you interested in her? You didn't know her, and she passed a long time ago." He said it pleasantly, and if he looked perplexed, well, I understood.

"I'm doing some research."

"On that murder, the one involving the colored serviceman. I know." So he had heard about me. "But that doesn't explain why you want to ask about my daughter."

He set down his cigarette, pulled a handkerchief from a pocket and wiped his eyes.

"Excuse me." He didn't offer to explain, but he didn't have to. Not only had a stranger turned up uninvited at his house, but that stranger—me—was asking about a painful past. He had already been a widower when his daughter died. Because of that, I felt I owed him an explanation.

But what could I say? Where should I start? The part about why I was writing the story? The part about me being an orphan? The part about Mrs. Hazelton and her envelopes? And what if Ellie Chisholm had been like Anne Tyler? What if she'd sneaked down to the Rooster and her father never suspected? What if, after mourning her for so long, imagining her in all her perfection, I told him something that marred that picture? How much would he hurt then?

Mr. Chisholm gazed out over his magnificent lawn.

"She was a quiet girl," he said. "Like her mother. Sweet too. Always considerate of others. I sent her away to a school with the nuns. To keep her safe."

His eyes seemed fixed on a point in the distance, as if it were the exact location of the piece of history he was telling me now.

"It was the same school her mother went to. It's not far from here, but far enough that she stayed there most weekends and engaged in wholesome activities, unlike so many youngsters around here at the time. I was going to send her to Switzerland, to a finishing school, but that didn't happen."

He turned to look at me.

"I've wondered many times over the years if I shouldn't have kept her at home. Family tradition is well and good, but at the end of the day, all it meant is that I hardly ever saw her. My most enduring memories of her are as a little girl, before she left for school. It wasn't until after she died that I realized I'd never gotten to know her as the fine young lady she was becoming."

"I'm sorry." I really was. I thought of leaving it at that. You bet I did. How do you ask a man if his sainted daughter, his nun-reared darling, associated with the victim of the first and last murder case in decades? Believe it or not, that's when Nellie flashed into my mind. I thought about all the things she had done, all the questions she had asked, all the people she had tracked down and interviewed, all with one purpose: to get the story.

I drew in a deep breath. "Sir, do you know if your daughter was friendly with a man named LaSalle?"

"LaSalle?" He shook his head. "The only LaSalle I know—and even then I can't say that I knew the man—was the fellow they found in the river. The one who was murdered. I can't remember his given name."

"It was Patrice. He's the person I mean."

Mr. Chisholm frowned. "My Ellie had nothing to do with him. She would never have had anything to do with a murder victim." He made it sound as if the victim were every bit as reprehensible as the killer.

"She never mentioned his name?"

"Not that I recall. Certainly not."

I took another sip of lemonade to be polite and then stood up.

"I'm sorry to have bothered you, sir."

"Is that it?" His voice rose in surprise. "Is that all you wanted to know?" Suddenly he was on his feet, towering over me. His pink cheeks had turned red. "Who are you doing this research for? Who's paying you? Why are you asking about my daughter?"

"I just—" I just what? Liked sticking my nose into other people's business and stirring up painful memories?

"My daughter died tragically young." He stepped a half pace closer to me, crowding me, but I couldn't make myself step back. "I spent a lifetime building a business so that I could give her everything she needed. She wanted for nothing, and I intended to keep it that way. Then she died. She'd just turned nineteen. She was a child. My baby girl."

Every reflex I had was telling me to leave, immediately, that I never should have come here and upset this man. But I was overawed by the size and opulence of his home. Should I go back the way I had come, through the house? Or would that get me into more trouble? Should I flee across the lawn? I couldn't tell for sure, but a garage seemed to be blocking one side, and flower beds the other.

Mr. Chisholm settled the matter. He picked up a bell; it looked like a schoolteacher's bell, the kind that Mrs. Hazelton rang to assemble us, except it was silver. He shook it and, like a genie in a puff of smoke, Alice appeared.

"Please see Miss Andrews out," Mr. Chisholm said.

Alice looked disapprovingly at me. It was clear that I had upset her employer. I wanted to apologize to Mr. Chisholm, but I couldn't find words that seemed adequate for the job. I fell into step beside Alice. She marched me through the kitchen, down the hall and to the big front door. I thought about explaining to her what had happened. But suddenly we were at the door. Alice held it open for me, her stance making it clear that she was in a hurry to close it again.

The ride back to town seemed longer and hotter than the ride to Mr. Chisholm's farm, and I berated myself for not drinking all of the lemonade before leaving. I couldn't help but wonder how the others from the Home were doing. Had any of them followed their clues to a living, breathing parent? Had any of them had a joyous reunion? Did they like what they'd found out? Were they glad they'd looked? Even if they were, that didn't mean that I would be. And what good did it do to think about that anyway? Take off your orphan hat, I told myself, and put on Nellie Bly's bonnet. Think, Cady. What are the facts as you know them?

I had more questions than answers.

All files relating to the arrest and prosecution of Thomas Jefferson were missing. By all files, I meant all the newspaper files and all the police files, except for the photos that were delivered to me at Maggie's house. I couldn't prove it, but the more I thought about it, the more sure I was that it was the cleaning woman from the sheriff's office who had brought them. But where had she found them if all the files were destroyed in the flood back in 1949?

Then there were the photos themselves. They suggested a different story from the one I had been told. They made it clear that Mr. LaSalle's body wasn't anchored to the pulley with rope. It was attached by cable. Cable doesn't rot or get nibbled by fish or fray to the point of breaking as a result of rubbing against rocks in a river. Whoever put that cable around Patrice LaSalle before they dumped him into the river wanted him to stay hidden in the depths, not float to the surface. The other thing about the cable: I didn't see how it could have been broken, not the way it looked. The photos showed a neat cut, not a ragged break. Someone must have cut that cable. But who? And why? And why did everyone insist that the body had been held in place by rope?

What about the confession? The only person who had supposedly heard it was Sheriff Beale. And even though the sheriff couldn't produce a signed confession in court and, more important, even though Mr. Jefferson insisted he had never confessed, the judge allowed the sheriff's testimony about it to be admitted as evidence against Mr. Jefferson. Maybe Mr. Jefferson's lawyer had done his best to present his case, but from what Daniel had told me, it didn't sound like it. If I could have read the trial transcript, I would have known exactly what had been said and by whom. But the transcript, like everything else, was missing. Without it, I had no way of knowing how impartial—or not—the trial had been.

And then there was the fact that several people had told me Mr. Jefferson had gone around town after Mr. LaSalle went missing, asking people if they'd seen him. Why would he do that if he'd already killed Mr. LaSalle? Why make a point of his absence? Why not just say that Mr. LaSalle had gone home to Canada?

And, finally, there was Sheriff Beale himself, the only person who'd heard Mr. Jefferson's supposed confession, living out his days in a nursing home complete with a private nurse that he couldn't afford. What, if anything, did that have to do with his testimony and with the missing police files? Were his bills being paid in return for perjured testimony or for making sure that key documents went missing?

Put all those facts together, and they raised yet another question—a big one: If Mr. Jefferson didn't murder Mr. LaSalle, who did? And why?

Was Mr. LaSalle killed simply to frame Mr. Jefferson for murder? If so, the killer had to be someone who hated that Mr. Jefferson, a black man, wanted to be treated like everyone else. A lot of people had complained about that. Mr. Selig had all but foamed at the mouth.

Or had someone killed Mr. LaSalle because they didn't like that he was friends with Mr. Jefferson? That couldn't be it, could it? This wasn't the south. As far as I knew, Indiana had never had slavery. So how could it be such a crime for two people with different-colored skin to be friends and go into business together?

I didn't have any answers.

But suppose Daniel and his mother were right. Suppose Mr. Jefferson hadn't killed Mr. LaSalle. Suppose someone else had done it. Someone like Mr. Selig. Or like the men who had followed me back to Maggie's. And suppose Mr. Jefferson had been mistakenly arrested or—this was also possible—suppose he'd been framed. Suppose certain evidence had been destroyed and other evidence manufactured—to make Mr. Jefferson look guilty. Wouldn't Sheriff Beale have to have been involved in that? If he was, and if he had any files or photographs or other information about what had really happened, he wouldn't have kept them in police files. That would have been foolhardy. And if that was true…

Was I being logical? Or was I grasping at straws because I wanted to believe Mrs. Jefferson and Daniel and because I didn't like the way some people in town talked about Mr. Jefferson? It was so confusing.

If Sheriff Beale had helped to cover up the truth about Patrice LaSalle's murder, and if Mrs. Jefferson was right when she insisted that Mr. Jefferson had never confessed, that meant Sheriff Beale had lied on the witness stand. A sheriff who would lie under oath might do a lot of other unsavory things. He might also take measures to make sure that no one would ever point the finger at him. He might have kept some information as insurance. Maybe he'd even used it to make sure that he was well rewarded for what he had done. It was possible. If he had, where would that information be now?

Did he take it home? He had a house in town. Mr. Standish had told me so. But where was it? Who would know? Who could I ask?

How about Sheriff Hicks? He would know.

I went back to the sheriff's office and found his secretary, two police officers doing paperwork, and the cleaning lady. Sheriff Hicks wasn't there. I approached his secretary instead and asked for Sheriff Beale's address.

"I'm sorry," she said. "But I can't help you."

"You don't know where his house is?"

"I don't give out personal information."

"But he doesn't live there anymore."

"I don't give out personal information." She crossed her arms over her chest and looked implacably at me. She was not going to budge.

I glanced at the two police officers at their desks behind her. They both looked away immediately. They were going to be no help either.

Chapter Eighteen

I GO INTO THE WOODS

I WAS STANDING on the sidewalk outside the sheriff's office, wondering who else would know where Sheriff Beale's house was, when I heard an urgent *Pssst!* The cleaning lady beckoned from the side of the building. She held up her hand, and I saw that she was holding a piece of folded paper. She dropped it and disappeared. I took a quick look around before retrieving it and stuffing it into my pocket. I didn't read it until I was well out of sight of the police station. An address was neatly printed on it. I walked a few more blocks before stopping a woman and asking for directions.

Sheriff Beale's house was not at all what I had expected. For one thing, it wasn't as old and staid as the other houses on the street. Instead of being two stories with a wraparound verandah, the house was a sleek, low-slung bungalow with a two-car garage. Everything looked new.

I was halfway up the front walk when a woman came out the front door with a baby on her hip.

"Can I help you?" she asked.

Everyone spoke so politely in Orrenstown. But few people had actually managed to help me. Maybe this time it would be different.

I asked her how long she had lived in the house.

"Since it was built."

I checked the address on the piece of paper. "I thought someone else used to live here."

"That's right. We tore down the old place after we bought it. It was a mess. It hadn't been lived in for a couple of years. We rebuilt completely."

Which meant another dead end. Unless...

"Was there anything left in the house when you bought it?" I asked.

The baby started fussing, and the woman jiggled it up and down in her arms.

"Only a few moldy old sticks of furniture and the most disgusting refrigerator you've ever seen. And the bathroom!" She shuddered. "I know the man who owned the place lived alone, but that's no excuse for the state of that bathroom."

"You didn't find any old papers or files?"

The woman shook her head. The baby squished up its face and fussed in its mother's arms.

"What about the people who demolished the old house? Did they find anything?"

"Honestly, I don't know." The baby started to cry in earnest. "Maybe you should talk to the woman who owned the house."

"Woman?" That didn't sound right. "You said a man lived here."

"Yes, but it was his daughter who sold the place. The real-estate agent told us that the old man was in a nursing home. The daughter put the house on the market. Apparently—and this is according to the real-estate agent—the house was in the daughter's name." She was holding the baby so that it could rest its head on her shoulder, but the baby was in no mood for that. He bellowed. "If you want to know anything else," his harried mother said, "you should talk to the daughter."

"Do you know how I can get in touch with her?"

The woman shook her head.

"Look," she said, "if I don't get this little man settled down before the sitter arrives, I'm going to miss my hair appointment. And if that happens, all kinds of other things are going to go wrong."

She took the squalling baby into the house.

It was possible, I thought, that Sheriff Beale's daughter had found some old files. She was the one who had put the house up for sale. She must have cleaned it out first. Or had it cleaned out. I knew from Mr. Standish that she didn't have much to do with her father, so the chances that she had kept any old records of his seemed remote. But you never know—not until you ask, that is.

But who would tell me where to find her? I didn't know her last name; all I knew was that she was the former sheriff's daughter and that she was married and had a daughter of her own.

The newspaper files!

I raced past Maggie, who was at her typewriter in her office off the kitchen, and straight down to the morgue in the basement. I didn't bother about the stacks of old newspapers. I went straight to the files. To the *B* drawer.

I found a file for *L. Beale*, but—no surprise—although it was stuffed with clippings, there was nothing about the arrest, trial or conviction of Thomas Jefferson. There was nothing about his personal life either.

But there was another Beale. *J. Beale*.

J for Jane.

Jane Beale, daughter of county sheriff Lorne Beale, was engaged to marry Michael Wellington, a corporate lawyer residing in Hartford, Connecticut. I copied down the information and went back upstairs.

I stood in the doorway to Maggie's office until she looked up from her work.

"I need to make a long-distance call," I said. "I'll pay you back."

Maggie just smiled. "Go ahead."

I used the phone in the front hall and called directory assistance to ask for the phone number of Michael Wellington in Hartford. There were two numbers: one for his office and one for his home. I wrote down both.

I dialed the home number first. A woman answered.

"Mrs. Wellington?"

"May I tell her who is calling?"

"My name is Cady Andrews."

"One moment, please."

I heard footsteps fading at the other end of the line. A moment later I heard them again. This time they were getting louder.

"I'm sorry," said the voice at the other end of the line. "Mrs. Wellington says she doesn't know anyone by that name."

"Can you please tell her it's about her father?"

I heard more footsteps. A different voice, an angry voice, came on the line. "If this is about that photograph, I don't know anything. I've never seen it."

What photo was she talking about? One of the three that had been slipped under Maggie's kitchen door?

I knew I had to talk fast, so I introduced myself and told her (I assumed I was speaking to the former Jane Beale) that I was looking for some old papers that Sheriff Beale may have had at his house.

"What kind of papers?" Her voice was heavy with suspicion.

"Files."

There was a long pause, and I braced myself for more questions.

"There were no files," Mrs. Wellington said decisively. "No files. No photograph. Just stacks of hunting magazines and old newspapers."

"The local newspaper?" I thought about the issues that were missing from Maggie's basement.

"It may have been. I didn't pay much attention. They were old."

"What did you do with them?"

"I threw them out." There was another pause. "Who did you say you were? Why are you asking these questions?"

"It's about the Jefferson murder trial."

"Jefferson?"

"The victim was a Patrice LaSalle."

"I don't know anything about that. I haven't lived in Orrenstown in a long time. So if there's nothing else—"

The phone went dead. Mrs. Wellington had hung up.

I put down the phone and went back to the kitchen to clean up the lunch dishes, which were still in the sink. While I washed and rinsed, I thought about the missing files. Maybe they'd been destroyed in the flood like Sheriff Hicks had said. Or maybe Sheriff Beale had taken them home. If he had, it was clear that they were gone now.

Most likely they'd been destroyed.

I let the water out of the sink and started to dry the dishes. Everything else related to the Jefferson case was missing. Somebody had done a thorough cleanup.

Then I remembered Sheriff Beale's cabin.

Mr. Standish had mentioned it. He'd said that Sheriff Beale had a cabin somewhere in the area. I wished I'd asked Mrs. Wellington about it. Should I call her back? If I did, would she talk to me again? Or was there another way to find out where that cabin was?

Mrs. Wellington had sold her father's house. Mr. Standish had said she would probably sell the cabin.

I finished drying the dishes and putting everything away. I called to Maggie that I had to go out but would do some chores later. Then I race-walked downtown, despite the sweltering afternoon heat, and made directly for the real-estate office on the main street. If someone here had handled the sale, there would be records. A bell tinkled over the door when I opened it, and I was hit with a blast of cold air that immediately set me shivering. The office was empty except for one woman at a desk. I recognized her. It was Helen, the friendlier of the two women from the diner.

She recognized me too.

"You're that girl," she said.

"Cady."

"What can I do for you, Cady? Surely you're not interested in buying real estate."

"I was talking to a woman a little while ago. She bought a house here, tore it down and built a new house. I think she said that the old sheriff used to live in the house."

"Lorne Beale's house?" Helen looked surprised. "Why are you interested in that?"

"I'm not, really. But I heard he also had a cabin somewhere. I was wondering if that had been sold too."

She was still smiling, but I had the feeling that something had changed. But what?

"I think I know the place you mean." She got up and went to a filing cabinet. She opened a drawer, thumbed through it and pulled out a folder. "Here is it. Yes, one of our agents represents it. But it hasn't been sold." She scanned the file. "The place is pretty old and run-down. Looks like it was used primarily as a hunting cabin. We haven't had any interest in it." She flipped the folder shut and looked expectantly at me.

"Can you tell me where it is?"

"Are you interested in purchasing it?"

"I've been telling my parents about Orrenstown. My father asked me to see if there were any vacation properties around."

"Oh?" I don't think I imagined the dollar signs in her eyes. But she hesitated. She already knew I was interested in Thomas Jefferson, and heaven only knew what else she had heard about me. But she opened the folder again and pulled out a sheet of paper, which she handed to me. There was a picture of a cabin at the top—a basic wood-framed, rectangular, one-story place. If it had ever been painted, the paint had long since baked or peeled off. I read the description: two rooms plus an outhouse, woodstove, shed for storing equipment, no electricity but there was a generator. The last paragraph gave directions from town.

"Is it far?" I asked. "I'd like to see it."

"It depends on how you plan to get there. Go to the north end of town. Then take the county road to a junction about five miles north. From there, follow the directions until you get to a dirt road. It's another couple of miles from there."

In other words, too far to walk. I'd have to go back to Maggie's and borrow her bicycle.

I thanked Helen and was on my way to the door when the bell above it jingled again and Mr. Selig walked in. Helen greeted him and asked what she could do for him.

I pedaled. And pedaled. And pedaled some more. The air seemed especially heavy. The sky was blue, but fluffy, white clouds were gathering in towers in the sky. I was drenched in sweat long before I reached the junction that the real-estate woman had told me about. I made a turn and found myself on a dirt road that had a surface like a never-ending washboard. It was almost impossible to ride on—the bike bounced up and down, and every bone in my body rattled. I kept going until I reached the woods and a twisty path that was thick with tree roots, rocks and windfall. I left the bike half hidden in some scrub near a stand of birch and marked the location by setting a small rock on top of a larger one, so that I'd be able to find it again.

From there it was into the woods. It was tough going. In one place, I had to scramble over a rock outcrop. But the air was cool under the trees, as only dapples of sunlight managed to penetrate the canopy overhead. It would be so easy to get turned around and hopelessly lost.

Helen had said the cabin was a couple of miles from the dirt road, but it felt to me as if I'd been walking for an eternity. I scanned ahead for anything resembling a cabin.

Nothing.

No, wait—there was something. A building.

A cabin.

It was sturdier than it looked in the picture. Its wood clapboard had been weathered by the elements, but every upright was true, every shingle was in place, and nothing sagged. The windows were dirt-streaked, and I had to rub hard with the heel of my hand to get a look inside. But the grime was even thicker on the inside of the glass, so I couldn't see much.

I tried the door. It was unlocked. At first that surprised me. But once I stepped inside, I got it. There was nothing worth stealing.

I began my search.

I looked under and behind every stick of furniture. I opened every cupboard, box and trunk. I peered inside, under and behind the box of wood next to the fireplace. I poked in, behind and under the box of kindling next to the wood-burning stove in the kitchen. I was just as thorough in the two small bedrooms. I searched everywhere. There were no files.

Two small buildings stood behind the cabin. One was down the path, almost out of sight around a bend.

The outhouse. A great place to hide something, because, honestly, even Nellie Bly would flinch at the thought of searching an outhouse. The other little building was much closer. I headed there first. Unlike the cabin, the door to this little building was secured with an enormous padlock. I shook, tugged, pulled, jerked and twisted that lock. It refused to give.

I circled the shed. There was a small window at the back, secured by a semicircular latch. I tried the window again. The latch wobbled, and the window slid up a fraction of an inch. I jiggled it again, and the latch slipped a little more. On my third attempt, the latch slid free of its mooring, and I was able to open the window all the way. Problem number one was solved. Now for problem number two.

The window was small. A child could have climbed through, but I wasn't a child anymore. I braced my hands on the inside of the sill and started to pull myself through.

I got stuck. The window frame caught me and held me as tightly as a girdle. There was nothing inside that I could grab onto. I kicked and wriggled. I even tried to push myself back out again. Nothing worked. I found myself fighting panic. What if I couldn't free myself? I hadn't told Maggie where I was going. Helen knew, but would she mention my interest in the cabin to anyone? What if I starved to death out here? What if—the thought sprang unbidden and unwelcome to my mind—what if a wild animal came along, a bear or a wolf or a big cat of some kind (did they have big cats down here?) and chomped on my bare legs? What if it started to eat me?

I sucked in my breath and held it, as if that would make my hips narrower. I wriggled and writhed until I was aglow with sweat. One hip bone grated against the rough window frame before finally popping through, and I fell headfirst to the dusty wood floor.

The interior of the small shed was gray and gloomy. The window didn't let much light in for the simple reason that there wasn't much light in the first place. The shed was surrounded by trees, and the tree canopy all but blocked out the sun. I wished I'd thought to bring a flashlight. I waited for a few moments until my eyes adjusted to the dimness, and then I searched, running my hands lightly over shelves and pieces of equipment. I didn't want to miss a thing.

The shed was filled with rusted leghold traps—I wondered what the sheriff had trapped out here—old jars of nails and screws, a box with some old hinges in it, some tools (a pick, a shovel, two hammers and what looked like a bolt cutter), lengths of chain and some empty crates. There were no files that I could see—or feel.

Getting back out through the small window was as difficult and scary as coming in. What if I got stuck now with my head and arms outside? What if a bear decided to nibble on my head? But I writhed and squirmed my way through. For sure there were going to be gigantic bruises on my hips.

That left one other building: the outhouse. I followed the path to the little structure, sucked in a deep breath and went inside. I even felt under the seat. Yuck! No files.

And that was that. This cabin was the last place I could think of to look for the missing police files on Thomas Jefferson—if they still existed.

Clearly, they didn't. And seriously, if you were going to commit perjury in a murder trial, why would you keep the evidence that proved you'd lied? Answer: you wouldn't. You'd destroy it. That way no one could ever prove anything. So of course Sheriff Beale had destroyed it.

I trudged up the path back to the cabin, shoulders slumped in discouragement, knowing with certainty that I was never going to get to the bottom of what had happened. All the evidence was missing. It had happened too long ago now. And even if there had been a miscarriage of justice, no one seemed to care.

That's when I noticed something at the rear of the cabin: a small trapdoor set at an angle in the ground. The door to a cellar.

My hand trembled when I reached for the handle. I lifted the door to reveal a set of wooden steps. My whole body felt electric with anticipation. I climbed down into darkness. The cellar was not large. It was square and just deep enough that I could stand tall and still have a couple of inches to spare over my head.

The cellar, it turned out, was also empty.

Except for five barrels along the back wall.

Barrel number one was empty.

So was barrel number two.

Barrel number three was home to a mouse that scampered up and out, startling me so that I dropped the lid.

Barrel number four was empty.

Barrel number five was stuffed with old greasy rags. I plucked them out one by one. Was there anything else in there? I reached way down, praying there wouldn't be a snake or a rat or more mice at the bottom. My fingers made contact with something hard. A box. I grabbed it by one corner and lifted it out.

It was a metal lockbox. A padlocked box.

I carried it up the steps and into the daylight.

When I shook it, I was sure I heard papers inside. I examined the lock. It was smaller than a regular padlock. I thought about that bolt cutter in the shed and sighed.

It took a full twenty minutes to get back into the shed, grab the bolt cutter and escape once more. I cut the lock easily, opened the box and took out two file folders. I sank down onto the nearest rock and began to flip through them.

Chapter Nineteen

I FIND SOMETHING UNEXPECTED—AND HORRIFIC

THERE WERE TWO file folders inside the metal lockbox. One was thick with paper and photographs—crime-scene photographs. I read everything—police reports, forms, notes, notes attached to forms, lists of people interviewed.

The second folder was so thin that at first I thought it was empty.

It wasn't.

There was a photograph inside. Just one. Black and white. Old. With a scrawl in faded ink on the back. I stared at it and remembered Mrs. Wellington saying, *I don't have that picture. I've never even seen it*. Was this the picture she meant? Did it have anything to do with what happened to Thomas Jefferson?

I had to take these file folders back to town. I planned to show the first one to Maggie. She would know what to do. I wasn't sure about the second one. I wasn't even sure that it really was what it appeared to be.

I made sure to leave everything exactly as I'd found it before I headed back down the winding path toward Maggie's bicycle. I was almost there when I heard voices.

"Where do you think she went?" one asked.

"There's only one place she could have gone," another voice said.

She? They had to mean me. Someone was looking for me. But how did they know I was here? Had Helen told them? Had Mr. Selig been curious about what I was doing at the real-estate office? Had he asked her?

I retreated back up the path to think. If those men knew where I'd gone, they would be coming my way soon. I could leave the path and head into the woods. But I wasn't confident that I'd be able to find my way out again. I knew how easy it was to get disoriented in unfamiliar woods.

I looked around frantically and spotted a fallen log a couple of feet away from the path. I ran to it and hid the file folders underneath it. Before I covered them with leaves, I took a note from the first folder and the photo from the other. These I slid under my blouse, anchoring them in the waistband of my skirt. Then I ran back to the path. I dug a medium-sized rock from the ground and set it beside a tree close to the log. I headed back to my bike.

Two men were waiting for me at the edge of the woods. One was examining Maggie's bicycle as if it could tell him where I'd gone and when I might return. The other was smoking a cigarette and peering in among the trees. He was the one who saw me first. I recognized him as one of the men in the mob that had followed me to Maggie's.

"Well, lookie here, Reg," he said to his companion. He was tall with a big belly and bow legs. The underarms of his short-sleeved shirt were drenched with sweat. "What are you doing way out here, little lady?"

I didn't answer him.

"My friend asked you a question," the other man said. He was shorter and wirier than his partner. "It's only polite to answer."

Right. Like their mission in life was to teach me good manners.

"I was taking a walk. That's my bike."

I didn't expect him to hand it over to me, and he didn't.

"A girl could get lost in those woods if she isn't careful," Cigarette Man said.

"I think I did okay," I said. "I got back where I started."

"Where did you go exactly?" That was the man holding Maggie's bike.

"For a walk. I have to get back to town. Miss Nearing is expecting me. She'll worry if I'm late."

The two men exchanged glances. Cigarette Man shook his head, as if I had somehow disappointed him. Bicycle Man said, "What were you doing in there, darlin'? Were you looking for something?"

I heard a crunching noise. Tires on gravel. A car door slammed, and Sheriff Hicks appeared, his hat shoved back on his head, eyes hidden behind dark glasses.

"Do we have a problem here, fellas?" His tone was genial. His thumbs were hooked into his belt, and one hand was close to his service revolver.

"Could be," Cigarette Man said. "If this young lady was trespassing on private property."

I couldn't see Hicks's eyes, but I knew he was studying me.

"Were you?" he asked.

"No, sir. I don't think so."

"Terrific. So we don't have a problem after all." He glanced at the bike. "That looks like Maggie's."

"It is."

Hicks took it from Bicycle Man. "I'll throw it into the trunk and give you a lift home."

I didn't argue. I couldn't wait to get away from here. But what about the files? Should I wait until the two men left and then go back and get them? Or should I leave them where they were for now?

Hicks looked at the two men. "Unless you have other business here..."

I guess they didn't want any trouble with Hicks, because they shuffled off in the direction of the road, and I heard an engine roar to life.

Hicks turned to me. "What *are* you doing out here?"

I hesitated. If I was going to tell anyone what I'd found, it should be Sheriff Hicks. But a question nagged at me. How had he known I was here? Or *had* he known? Maybe he was just driving by and saw the car or the truck or whatever those two guys were driving and decided to investigate. It was possible. It was also possible that his appearance was no coincidence. I remembered that he hadn't exactly been helpful so far. If anything, he had been downright forgetful. I decided not to tell him about my discovery. Not yet anyway.

"I was exploring the woods," I said. "It sure beats Central Park."

Hicks nodded as if he was satisfied with my answer, and we set off for his patrol car. He stowed the bike in the trunk and secured the trunk lid with a piece of rope.

"A person can get lost in the woods if they don't know what they're doing," he told me as he turned the car around. "You have a compass?"

"No."

He glanced at me. "Did those two fellas give you a hard time?"

"They scared me a little." I hadn't told him about the mob that had followed me. I wondered if anyone else had.

"That's another reason to stay out of the woods. You run into any trouble, and you're on your own."

"You don't think they would have hurt me, do you?"

"I think a girl should never go into strange woods by herself, especially if she doesn't tell anyone where she's headed. You never read that story about Little Red Riding Hood? You're lucky I came along when I did."

He was right about that.

"Do you come out here often?" I asked.

"It's part of my patrol. And when I see a pickup truck belonging to a couple of fellas like those two, well, I stop and take a look-see."

It made sense. But it still rankled. His timing couldn't have been better.

When we got to Maggie's, he unloaded the bike and said, "Your family must be missing you. Don't you think you should be heading home?"

Chapter Twenty

A PHOTO, A NOTE AND A KILLER

I DIDN'T KNOW what to do. I had to retrieve those folders from the woods, but I wasn't about to go back there now, not when there was a chance those two men might be lurking around. I told myself that as long as it didn't rain, the folders would be safe where they were. I glanced up at the sky. The clouds had massed and grown taller since the last time I'd looked up. But they were white, so I wasn't worried.

In the meantime, I needed to talk to someone about what I had found. Maggie was the only person I trusted, but she was out covering a story and wouldn't be back for hours. Besides, she'd lived away from Orrenstown for a long time.

I grabbed the telephone directory and looked up a name and an address.

Mr. Standish lived on a street where all the houses were made of brick and had wraparound porches, gingerbread trim and lush lawns surrounded by hedges and fences. The driveway was long and led to a garage that was set back even farther from the road than the house was. Mr. Standish was standing in front of the open garage door when I got there. He was wearing safety goggles and sharpening a hoe. His pickup was parked inside. Next to it was a workbench. Tools hung on the wall, each one in its own bracket. A small door at the back of the garage gave me a glimpse of the backyard.

Mr. Standish looked up.

"What a surprise." He pushed the goggles up over his forehead and smiled at me. "To what do I owe this visit?"

I dug in my pocket and pulled out the black-and-white photograph. I handed it to him.

Mr. Standish stared at it for a long time. "Where did you get this?"

"That's Sheriff Beale," I said. I pointed to a figure on the far right. "That's Mr. Chisholm. And I'm sure you recognize your friend here." I jabbed a finger at Mr. Selig. "They look pretty young in that picture, but that's them."

Mr. Standish's nod was almost imperceptible. His eyes remained fixed on the photo for another few seconds. He didn't say a word when he handed it back to me.

"Do you know anything about this, Mr. Standish?"

This was a shocking picture. In it, a man—a black man—was suspended from a tree by a rope around his neck. His eyes were closed, and his head lolled to one side. His hands were tied behind his back, and he was surrounded by people.

I wasn't positive, but I had a strong hunch that he was TJ's father. The people in the foreground—there were ten of them, all men, all white—looked directly at the camera. Worse, they smiled for it.

Mr. Standish shook his head. "I heard about what happened. But I wasn't there."

He glanced over his shoulder. I heard the sound of a lawn mower coming from somewhere behind the house. He must have someone helping him with his yard work. Probably a local kid earning pocket money.

"It's an old story." Mr. Standish stared out over his front yard—the grass, the elm tree, the trimmed hedge, the stone path to the verandah. "A woman—a white woman—said she was accosted by a Negro man. She described him. He was arrested. Her husband was incensed and demanded that something be done. The next thing you know, there was a mob. This was back in, let me see, '31, I think. The Depression had started. Times were tough. And people thought differently then."

It definitely sounded like the story Daniel had told me.

"But you can't hang a person for accosting someone." The idea was shocking.

"You can't do it legally, no," Mr. Standish said. "It was a mob. The sheriff, Sheriff Beale, had to go out of town on business that evening. Or so he said. If I'm not mistaken, he made his getaway just about the time one of his deputies told him that a crowd was forming in the town square. The two deputies who were on duty swear they did their best to control the crowd. They claim they did everything short of shooting, and as one of them put it, there was no way they were going to shoot their friends and neighbors over something like that, by which I assume they meant over a mob trying to get its hands on a Negro man who had assaulted a white woman."

"Was anyone arrested?"

"There was an investigation. The sheriff—when he got back to town—questioned everyone he could find. There were a lot of people there, as you can see by that picture, but it's a funny thing. No one saw exactly what happened, no one got a clear enough look at anyone who was involved. No one knew where the rope came from or how it got around that poor man's neck."

"But this picture—"

"There were rumors about a picture, but it never surfaced. Where did you get it anyway?"

I dodged the question. "Who was he?"

"The man who was hanged?"

"Lynched."

"Lynched." He nodded as he said the word. "His name was William Jefferson."

"Thomas Jefferson's father." Just as I had guessed.

"A lot of folks in Freemount moved away after that," he said. "But not Lila Jefferson. She stayed. She made accusations—which, of course, no one took seriously. She tried to get the FBI to investigate. They declined. She wrote letters to the NAACP, telling them what happened. But nothing came of it. I think a lot of people hoped that she would pack up and leave too. But she didn't. She stayed put. I'll tell you, it galled a lot of people when she'd walk down the street and, instead of looking away or stepping aside when a white person approached, stand her ground and look them in the eye. You'd think someone would have shoved her aside, but no one ever did. If you ask me, I think her presence here made people ashamed of what they'd done. I could be wrong, but it's the only reason I can think of that no one tried to force her out."

I couldn't believe what I was hearing.

"What about Mr. LaSalle?"

"What about him?"

"Do you know who killed him?"

Mr. Standish shook his head. "I only know what came out in court. And what happened before that."

"What do you mean?"

"The same kind of people who are in that photo didn't take too kindly to Jefferson coming back here a supposed war hero."

"Supposed?"

"Some people didn't believe him. Lyle Nearing, Maggie's father, did some research and ran an article in the paper backing up everything that Jefferson said. Some people will tell you that made things worse. They'll say it made Jefferson puff out his chest even more and strut about like a rooster in a henhouse. Those people made it tough for Jefferson whenever he came into town. Made it tough for his friend too."

"Do you think someone—someone white, I mean—killed Mr. LaSalle?"

Mr. Standish stared out over his lawn again for a long while before answering.

"I know that LaSalle stopped coming to town for a while before he disappeared."

"So people really thought he'd gone back home?"

Mr. Standish shook his head. "He showed up again after that. I never heard anything about where he'd been spending his time. When he went missing again, Jefferson looked for him all over. He must have asked everyone in town if they'd seen him."

"And that was used against him," I said. "Everyone thought he did that to cover up the murder."

"So they say. Then Brad Hicks found the body on his way to work one day. Jefferson was arrested. He confessed to murdering LaSalle. That's what Sheriff Beale testified to in court, under oath. And that's what got Jefferson convicted."

"Sheriff Hicks was on his way to work? So he wasn't looking for Mr. LaSalle?"

"As far as I know he wasn't. No one was. Why would they? If anyone thought about him at all, they assumed he went back to where he came from. At least, they did until Hicks found him."

“Did Sheriff Hicks live near where the body was found? Is that how he happened to find him?”

“Near?” He shook his head. “He lives about five miles out of town. Drives back and forth on the river road at least twice a day. Sometimes more often.”

The rest I already knew. I slipped the picture back into my pocket. As I did, I noticed that something had changed. The lawn mower had stopped. Mr. Selig was standing in the door to the garage, looking at us. I wondered how long he had been there.

Mr. Standish looked skyward, and I followed his gaze.

“There’s going to be one heck of a storm coming through here,” he said.

“Storm?”

“See those anvil heads?” He pointed at the clouds. “That means we’re going to have thunder, lightning, the whole nine yards.”

I thought of the folders I’d stashed under a layer of leaves. One was empty, since I’d taken the photograph. But the other one…It would get ruined in the storm. And if there was wind…

I had to go back and get it. Now. Before it rained.

I wished Maggie were home. I would tell her everything and get her to come with me. But I had no idea where she was.

I raced home and jumped on the bike. I flew over the paved roads to the junction, keeping watch that no one was following me. I didn’t see a single car or truck the whole way. I slowed down when I got to the turnoff and the washboard road. This time I hid the bike so well that there was very little chance of anyone finding it. I retraced my steps, my eyes searching the ground for my marker.

Something snapped in the underbrush behind me. I spun around and found myself face-to-face with Sheriff Hicks.

"What are you doing here?" I asked. Where had he come from? I was sure he hadn't followed me. Had he come back out here ahead of me? But why would he do that?

"I might ask you the same thing. Seems to me I just got you out of trouble out here. A smart girl would have stayed in town where she was safe."

"I—I guess you're right," I said. I turned to retrace my steps.

He caught me by the arm.

"Come on," he said. "Why don't you show me what you found?"

What I found? How did he know I found anything?

"You've been snooping around for days. Helen at the real-estate office told me you were asking about Lorne Beale's cabin. What did you find?"

"Find? Nothing. I just—I really have to go. Maggie will worry."

"Maggie's in Princeton. She won't be back until later tonight."

I tried to dart around him, but he caught me by the arm and held tight. Too tight. His fingers dug into my arm.

"Show me where you put it," he said. There was no smile on his face. No kindly concern for my well-being. He was deadly serious. He shoved me ahead of him. "Show me and I'll see that you get on a bus for New York City today."

The hardness in his eyes told me not to trust him.

I stumbled forward.

"No tricks now," he warned. He maintained his grip on my arm.

I kept walking, worried that I wouldn't be able to find the hiding place, until suddenly there it was, right in front of me, the rock I had set near the tree and, beyond it, the fallen log. They looked so obvious to me that they seemed to flash neon. I glanced at Sheriff Hicks. He didn't seem to have noticed anything.

I slowed my pace. I had to get that folder. I also had to get away from him.

Thunder grumbled overhead. Lightning illuminated the sky like a gigantic camera flash.

"I wrote everything down," I said. "I always write everything down. If anything happens to me, your secret will come out. Everyone will know what you did."

His lips curled in amusement.

"Is that right? And what is it that you think I did, little lady?"

"It's not what I think. It's what I know." I injected as much confidence as I could into my voice, but the truth was that I was shaking all over. He was a big man. With a gun. I was just me, Cady Andrews, aspiring intrepid reporter.

"Which is?"

"You lied about how you found Patrice LaSalle. And I think Sheriff Beale knew you lied. I think there was some kind of conspiracy going on to frame Thomas Jefferson for murder, and you were part of it."

He laughed.

"You're a real piece of work," he said. "I found LaSalle, all right."

"You drove back and forth along the river every day to get to work," I told him. "I've been there. I saw where the body was dumped. It's impossible to see anything in the river there. It's too muddy and too deep."

"There was a big storm. The body floated to the surface."

"No, it didn't. It couldn't have. It was secured to a pulley at the bottom of the river by a cable that was only a couple of feet long. There was no way it could have floated to the surface—unless someone cut the cable."

"Well then, I guess that's what happened," he said smoothly.

"You cut it." I was feeling more confident, thanks to the folder I'd found at the cabin. "The police reports say that the body was attached to the pulley with a rope, and that the rope broke. But that's not true. It was attached by a thick cable. I've seen pictures. There's no way that cable could have broken unless someone cut it. That's what you did. You knew where the body was. You cut the cable, retrieved the body, and then you and Sheriff Beale framed Thomas Jefferson for murder. But why? Because he wanted to be treated just like everyone else? Is that a crime around here?"

Sheriff Hicks was still smiling. He was still holding me in his grip.

I walked forward until I was almost on top of the file. With my next step, my ankle went out from under me. Kind of on purpose. I fell. I grabbed as much dirt as I could, and when Sheriff Hicks caught hold of my arm again and pulled me up, I threw the dirt into his eyes. He staggered back, cursing. I grabbed the folder and ran.

I ran as if my life depended on it. Because it did. I heard Sheriff Hicks bellow behind me, and I poured on the speed. I did my best to keep moving east, so I wouldn't lose my bearings. I leaped over tree trunks and rocks. I ducked under fallen branches. I kept running even when the rain started to patter on the overhead canopy. I was still running when the sky opened up with such fat, heavy raindrops that they tumbled through the foliage and beat against the ground below. I didn't stop running until the lightning started.

I had to get out from under all those trees.

I ran until I reached the extreme edge of the woods. I ran until I tripped on an exposed tree root and went flying, landing face down on rock and mud and slick leaves. Down and hurt and staring into an opening of some kind. A gap between some rocks. A little cave. I crawled inside and pulled some brush over the opening. Then I held my breath and waited.

I heard heavy breathing. I heard footsteps. I heard cursing. They grew loud and then faint again. I heard Hicks shouting my name in the distance.

The sky was black, lit now and again by sheet lightning. The rain hammered down. I clutched the folder to keep it dry. I started to shiver.

I don't know how, but despite the wind and the rain and the damp that seized me and held me like a giant wet, cold hand, I fell asleep. When I woke up, everything was quiet. Cautiously, I uncovered the opening of my cramped hiding place. The woods were dark save for a sliver of moonlight. I stayed put, barely breathing, until my eyes grew accustomed to the darkness and I was sure there was no one out there waiting for me. I crept out on my hands and knees and slowly unfolded myself and stretched. I was shaking all over from the cold and the damp. I knew I couldn't stay where I was. I had to get back to town.

There was no sign of Sheriff Hicks.

I stumbled around for what seemed like hours before I finally happened upon the trail again. Heaven knows I didn't find it as a result of searching for it, because the truth was that I had no idea where to look. I followed it back to the dirt road. Maggie's bike was exactly where I had left it. I climbed on and started to ride, scanning all around me, half terrified that Sheriff Hicks would appear out of nowhere, gun in hand.

He didn't.

When I got to the junction, I was more nervous than ever. What if he was waiting for me here? What if he was waiting just down the road or around the corner? What if...?

It was coming on dawn by the time I made my way to Freemount and knocked on Mrs. Jefferson's door. She didn't have a phone, but she dispatched Daniel to town to get Maggie while she fed me chicken and gravy with biscuits and a big glass of milk. I tried to make myself eat slowly, like the lady Mrs. Hazelton wanted me to be. But it was too hard. It had been more than thirty-six hours since I'd had anything to eat. And the thirst—down went the first glass of milk, followed swiftly by the second.

Daniel finally returned, Maggie in tow.

"The sheriff was sitting in his car outside Maggie's house," he reported. "I had to go around the back, and then I had to convince her to sneak out so he didn't see us." The impatient expression on his face told me this had not been easy.

"What on earth is going on?" Maggie asked when she saw me. "Where were you? I was so worried. And why do I have to slink around like a criminal?"

In answer to all her questions, I pushed the thick file folder across the table to her. She opened it and frowned, then she sat down and started to read. Mrs. Jefferson made coffee. Maggie sipped it gratefully while she worked her way through the file.

"Where did you get this?" She looked at me, a stunned expression on her face.

I told her the whole story.

"The only thing I can't figure out," I said, "is why he used cable instead of rope. It's like he didn't want the body to be found at all and then changed his mind. But why?"

But Maggie was focused on something else.

"Sheriff Beale lied." She looked at Mrs. Jefferson. "He lied. Your son never confessed."

Chapter Twenty-One

I CATCH A MURDERER

"HOW DO YOU know that? Show me." Mrs. Jefferson looked down at the file in front of Maggie. Maggie pointed, and Mrs. Jefferson and Daniel huddled around her and began to read.

"Sheriff Beale perjured himself." Maggie's expression was grim. "We have to take this to the police."

"No!" I practically shouted the word at her. "Sheriff Hicks was in on it." I told her what I had figured out. "It says in there that the body was secured by a rope and that the rope broke. But that's not true." I told her about the pictures that had been slipped under her kitchen door.

"That must have been Alma," Mrs. Jefferson said. "She cleans the municipal offices, including the sheriff's office. But where did she get them?"

It was a good question, one to which I didn't yet have the answer.

"They show that Mr. LaSalle was anchored to that pulley by a cable. Either someone cut that cable just before Hicks drove by—which doesn't seem likely, 'cause how would anyone else know he was coming?—or Hicks cut it himself."

"So he knew where the body was?" Daniel asked.

I nodded.

"Then he and Sheriff Beale lied about it and said the body had been secured with rope and that the rope had broken in the storm."

"Why would they do that?" Daniel asked.

That's the question that had been plaguing me.

"They wanted to get Thomas." Mrs. Jefferson looked at me, fire in her eyes. "They framed my son for murder."

"But why?" Maggie asks. "I'm not saying that's not what happened, but what did Hicks have against Thomas?"

"The same thing they all did. They hated him because he was a hero. And because he wanted to be treated like a man—like any man, not like a colored man."

Maggie glanced at me. Her voice was soft when she said, "Then—and I mean no offense, Mrs. Jefferson, I'm just saying—if their target was your son, why was LaSalle's body the one found in the river?"

"Because they couldn't stand that a white man was friends with him."

"Sheriff Beale was in on it too," I reminded them.

"Why would Beale lie to cover for Hicks?" Maggie frowned. "Hicks was a rookie back then. He wouldn't have been more than twenty-one or twenty-two."

"Maybe he did it as a favor," I said quietly.

"A favor to whom?"

I had thought long and hard about this. "To Mr. Chisholm."

"John Chisholm?" Maggie was thunderstruck. "What does he have to do with it?"

"I think his daughter was seeing Patrice LaSalle." There, I had said it out loud. "And Mr. Chisholm found out. I think he didn't approve because LaSalle was good friends with Mr. Jefferson." I paused. "And then there's this."

I slipped out the picture that I had already showed Mr. Standish. Maggie, Mrs. Jefferson and Daniel all stared at it.

"My God!" Maggie murmured. Then: "Excuse my language. Who is it? Do you know?"

"It's my first husband," Mrs. Jefferson said softly. "That's Thomas's father."

Maggie stared at her. Then she turned to me. "Where did you get this?"

"The same place I found this file."

"Beale had it?"

"There was always a rumor that someone had a picture," Mrs. Jefferson said. "But it never came to light."

"No wonder." Maggie couldn't take her eyes off it. She turned it over and looked at the scrawl on the back.

"I think that's why Sheriff Beale is in that fancy nursing home. He made sure no one went to jail for the lynching. I also think it's why his daughter broke with him," I said. "When I talked to her, she was angry because she thought I wanted to ask her about this photo."

"You spoke to Beale's daughter?" Maggie asked. "She must have told somebody about that. That might explain the trouble you had in the woods."

"Or Mr. Selig could have said something." I told them what had happened at Mr. Standish's. And pointed out that Mr. Selig was in the picture too.

"It hasn't been publicly announced yet, but John Chisholm is planning a run for governor," Maggie said softly. "If this picture comes out, that'll put an end to his political career before it evens starts."

"If there's any justice in the world, it should put him in prison," Mrs. Jefferson said.

"There's no statute of limitations on murder," Maggie said. "And if a lynching isn't murder, I don't know what is. You should talk to a lawyer, Mrs. Jefferson. You should get some advice on how to light the fire you need to get your husband's and your son's murderers brought to account." She stood up. "I have to go back to town. I have to make a phone call."

"Who are you going to call?"

"Not the sheriff's office, that's for sure. Cady, you stay here."

I stayed until late afternoon, when Maggie came back with two men in dark suits. They were from the Justice Department.

"I didn't know who else to call," Maggie said. "I didn't know who to trust."

The men sat me down at Mrs. Jefferson's kitchen table and made me go through everything again. Twice. And then once more for good measure. I told them everything I knew. I showed them the place in the report where someone—Sheriff Beale, it seemed—had written that the body was secured by rope. I showed them the pictures that the cleaning lady, Alma, had given me; Maggie had brought them from the house after I told her where they were hidden. I pointed out that in court, Sheriff Beale and Deputy Hicks had testified that Jefferson said LaSalle had left town. Then I showed them Sheriff Beale's initial notes, which he made after asking Jefferson when he'd last seen LaSalle. In the notes, Jefferson was recorded as saying he had no idea where his friend was and that he'd been asking all over town. Sheriff Beale even verified this by talking to the owner of the hardware store and to Mr. Selig. But when the report was typed up, after Jefferson was arrested, Sheriff Beale wrote that Jefferson had been telling everyone that LaSalle had left suddenly and gone home.

"That was a lie," I said.

The two Justice Department agents spent a long time on the older picture, the one of the lynching. They wanted to talk to Mrs. Jefferson too. Daniel and I sat together in the front room and waited. By the time they had finished, the sun was going down again. They told Maggie and me that they were going to arrest Sheriff Hicks on a charge of attempted kidnapping. They said that should keep me safe until they had a chance to go through everything thoroughly.

Chapter Twenty-Two

I GET MY STORY

IT WAS NO more than twenty-four hours later when Maggie came to get me and told me that Hicks was under arrest and that John Chisholm and Mr. Selig were under investigation for the lynching. The agents were trying to track down more information but had run into a *brick wall* (their words) with people in town who might have been around when the *incident* (also their word) occurred. They told me that with things the way they were down in Mississippi with the three young men who were missing in Neshoba County, the president himself was not inclined to be soft when it came to race relations.

"What about Patrice LaSalle's murder?" I asked.

The older of the two agents smiled.

"On top of the charges against Hicks relating to you," he said, "we have him dead to rights for perjury and tampering with evidence in a capital case. And those photos of LaSalle's body—the ones that show the body was tied down with cable and that the cable was cut—we sweated Hicks on that too."

"Did you talk to Alma, the woman who gave me the pictures?"

"She's been cleaning that office for a long time. She cleared out Sheriff Beale's stuff when he retired, and she found these pictures. But she didn't know what to do with them. She didn't trust the sheriff's office, not after the lynching. She didn't trust the authorities at all. She didn't know who to show them to—until you came along."

"And?"

The agent's smile widened to a satisfied grin. "At a minimum, that's accessory after the fact. Could even be conspiracy to commit murder. We put them all together for him, told him straight that we don't think we'll have much trouble finding a judge who will impose penalties for each crime consecutively instead of concurrently, in which case he could be in prison for the rest of his life, and—"

"And he cracked," the second agent said.

"He knows he's going away. He doesn't want to end up somewhere where there are a lot of black prisoners. He wants to make a deal—at the very least, he wants protective custody."

"And?" My heart was doing another sprint. Had they really gotten to the bottom of what happened?

"He gave up the murderer."

I glanced at Maggie. She didn't say anything.

"He says it was Chisholm," the older agent said. He gave Maggie a sharp look. "You remember our deal, right?"

"Not a word of anything you say gets reported until an arrest is made," Maggie said dutifully.

The older agent turned back to me. "Patrice LaSalle and Chisholm's daughter, Ellie, were seeing each other. Ellie kept it secret from her father because she knew how he felt about LaSalle, largely because he was friendly with Jefferson. But he found out. He says he went looking for him. Met up with him along the river, not far from where Hicks lives. Says when he told LaSalle to stay away from his daughter, LaSalle tried to blackmail him."

"Blackmail him?"

"That's what he says."

"How?"

"Didn't say. Wants to talk to a lawyer before he'll say another word. But Hicks says, from the looks of it when he got there—"

"Did Mr. Chisholm call him?"

The agent gave a wry smile. "That's the one chance thing. The only one. Hicks drove by on his way home and recognized Chisholm and stopped to see if he needed help. From what he says, it looks like Chisholm really went at the victim with a piece of pipe. Apparently, there was some old machinery abandoned down there at the time. Anyway, Hicks agreed to help him dispose of the body."

"With some of that old machinery—a pulley and some wire."

The agent nodded.

"Nobody was supposed to know what happened," he said. "The idea was that everyone would figure LaSalle had left town."

"That doesn't make sense. Why would he help dispose of the body?"

The agent sighed. "Hicks was in love with Ellie. He thought he was helping his future father-in-law get rid of the competition."

"So why did he cut the wire and then say he'd found the body? To frame Jefferson?"

"He says he did it when he found out that Chisholm had no intention of letting his daughter spend time with, much less marry, a nonentity like Hicks. He wanted to get even. So he cut the wire, 'found' the body and went to Beale with the discovery. He thought it would make him a hero to Ellie. He didn't figure that Chisholm had Beale in his pocket."

"What do you mean?"

"Chisholm contacted Beale. Beale made the cable disappear and replaced it with rope. And the two of them cooked up the idea of blaming Jefferson—anything to clear Chisholm. If Hicks went along, Chisholm guaranteed him that he'd back him for sheriff after Beale retired, which is exactly what happened the following year. Hicks claims he was also promised he could take his chances with Ellie. But before that could happen, she died."

Something clattered to the floor, making everyone jump. Mrs. Jefferson had dropped a pot.

"Then it really is true?" There were tears in her eyes. "My son really was innocent?"

"It looks that way, ma'am," the older agent said. "We just have to get all our ducks in a row, and then, I can assure you, there will be arrests, there will be prosecutions, and every effort will be made to clear your son's name."

Mrs. Jefferson began to weep in earnest. Daniel did his best to comfort her, but she said, "They're tears of joy, child. Tears of joy."

There was an almost immediate uproar in town. Mr. Chisholm was arrested and denied bail. The town was divided when the picture of the lynching was printed—in Maggie's newspaper, along with a feature article by Maggie. Some people were shocked. Others thought that because it had happened so long ago, it was best forgotten.

"There's no statute of limitations on murder," Maggie said grimly. "And Chisholm has been charged with two of them. Forget about his political career and his businesses—he's going to be locked up for the rest of his life."

Mrs. Jefferson kept thanking me. When I decided it was time for me to head back to Toronto to write my story, Mrs. Jefferson insisted on making me a farewell supper. It was a sumptuous feast—chicken and three kinds of vegetables, a garden salad, homemade pie and ice cream. I had never eaten so well or so much. Mrs. Jefferson hugged me and kissed me and told me that she'd never been so blessed to meet someone as she was when she met me. No one had ever said anything like that to me before.

I found Mr. Standish at home, drinking his morning coffee on his back verandah. He invited me to join him and asked if I was hungry. I shook my head and took a seat across from him at the little table. I pulled out the handwritten note I'd found attached to the medical examiner's report. I knew from all the other handwritten notes in the file that this particular one had been written by Sheriff Beale.

Mr. Standish scanned it. His face was expressionless when he handed it back to me.

"You're a doctor," I said. "A medical doctor."

"Was," he said.

"It says there that the coroner requested that you examine the body when it was found, but you refused."

"That's right."

I couldn't even begin to decipher his thoughts. There were no clues at all on his face.

"Why don't people call you doctor?" I asked.

"Because I'm retired. And because I don't like to be called that anymore."

"Why did you refuse to examine the body?"

"Because I didn't want to get involved."

I stared at him. He didn't want to get involved?

"Involved in what?"

"Involved in whatever happened to that man." He set down his coffee cup and laid one hand on each knee. "I knew the minute those two arrived in town that there was going to be trouble."

"Because of the lynching?"

"Because of how people felt about Jefferson. Because of the way he carried himself—justifiably, in my opinion. The man volunteered to go and fight in that war. He saw action, and, from what I heard, he acquitted himself well. It's a fact, even if people didn't like that."

"I don't understand." It had been baffling me ever since I'd arrived in town. "Why did people get so upset about someone who just wanted what everyone else had?" The most important of those things, I knew now, was respect.

"I've asked myself that question a thousand times, maybe more." He looked deep into my eyes, and I sensed there was something he wanted to tell me. But all he said was, "Some people think that the more someone else gets, the less there is for them."

"Did you know that Mr. Jefferson didn't kill Mr. LaSalle?"

"I suspected it. I couldn't think why he would. But there was nothing I could do about it. I couldn't prove anything."

"Maybe if you'd agreed to examine the body," I suggested.

"Maybe." He shook his head. "The way it works here, when a body is found, the sheriff calls the county coroner. In the state of Indiana, coroners are not required to be medical doctors, and most of them aren't. They're unqualified elected officials. And in this county, if you want to get elected, you're beholden to Mr. John Chisholm. It's up to the coroner whether or not to order an autopsy. Then it's up to him how to proceed from there. I didn't see the point of getting involved. All I would have discovered is that LaSalle had been murdered and dumped into the river."

"You might have found out something else," I said. I told him about the cable that had secured the body. "If you'd seen the body, you might have seen that Hicks lied."

Mr. Standish looked down for a long time. His expression was somber when he faced me again.

"I guess you could say that not only did I not want to get involved, but I also didn't want to know. I had a comfortable living here. Good patients. Decent remuneration for what I did. Nice house." He glanced around, and I had to agree: it was a nice house on a nice piece of property. The kind of house a lot of people dream of owning one day. "I don't mind telling you that I'm ashamed of myself. I was a coward, and I know it. But it was all in the past. No one talked about it anymore, and I was able to put it mostly out of my mind. And then you showed up."

I wanted to understand. In a way, I thought maybe I did. But I promised myself that I would never commit the same sin. I would never be afraid to do the right thing. I didn't want to go through life hating myself or regretting decisions I'd made. I got up to leave.

"Sit a minute," Mr. Standish said. "I want to tell you something."

Curious, I sat.

"It's about Ellie Chisholm. You know she was seeing LaSalle behind her father's back."

I nodded.

"She was completely hysterical when his body was found. Her father told her that he'd paid LaSalle off, that he gave him a lot of money to get out of town and leave her alone. I have no doubt she believed him. John Chisholm was a rich and powerful man then, and he's richer and more powerful now. Anyway, Chisholm called me to the house. He wanted me to give her a sedative. That's when I found out."

"Found out what?"

"She was pregnant."

I stared at him.

"She told me it was LaSalle's baby, but that her father didn't know yet. She made me promise not to tell her father, even though we both knew that it was only a matter of time before he found out. Sure enough, about two months later, Chisholm announced that he was sending Ellie away for a while, that she needed to get out of town after everything that had happened. She didn't come back for nearly a year."

"When she came back, did she have...?" I couldn't make myself finish the question.

"Did she have the baby with her? No. The baby was never mentioned, but later, when I did a routine physical examination of her, it was clear that she'd had the baby. I suppose she put it up for adoption."

I could hardly breathe.

"That would have been her father's decision," Mr. Standish said. "Not Ellie's. When she came back, she wasn't the same. She was thin and pale. She hardly ever left the house. She made several suicide attempts. And finally she succeeded. Of course, no one knows that. As far as anyone is concerned, her death was accidental." Before I could ask how that could be, he said, "I signed the death certificate." I leaned forward. "I didn't know who you were for sure until you headed for Freemount. You have your mother's coloring, but you resemble your father—quite a lot."

You resemble your father. Those were words that I never imagined I would hear.

"Do you really think...?" Again, I couldn't finish. It couldn't be true. Not after a whole lifetime of wondering.

"You could take a blood test. I have both of their blood types on record. But I'm as sure as I can be. You're the right age. And you look exactly like him."

I sat for a long time on Mr. Standish's porch. For a while we were both silent. I couldn't wrap my mind around what I'd just learned. Then Mr. Standish started talking again. He told me everything he knew about Ellie, which turned out to be a lot because he delivered her into the world. He told me about Ellie's mother and about John Chisholm. He knew so much about that family after having been their family doctor for a lifetime. He told me, too, what he knew about

Patrice LaSalle. It wasn't nearly as much, but it was a lot more than I'd known.

"He was a good man," Mr. Standish said. "A fair man. And he didn't let anyone change his mind about what he thought was right."

I drank in every word. When I got up to leave, Mr. Standish stood too, and before I could stop myself, I was hugging him.

"Thank you," I said. "Thank you so much."

There were tears in his eyes too, but I suspected that his were tears of regret.

I had my bag packed and was waiting for the Justice Department agents on Maggie's porch. Maggie came out of the house with something in a brown paper bag.

"Sandwiches for the ride home," she said. "And some cookies. Homemade."

I thanked her. There was no avoiding what I had to say, and it was now or never.

"About that picture, the one of the lynching," I began. "There was a stamp on the back of it, Maggie."

"I know. I saw it."

The stamp was in red ink and identified the photo as *Ledger* property.

"Daniel told me he once asked your father if he could go through old papers to find out about the lynching. He said he overheard his mother mention it," I told her. "Your father said okay. But when Daniel looked, there were papers missing. Just like there were papers missing for TJ's arrest and trial. It could be just a coincidence."

"Could be," Maggie said. She gazed out over the street before turning to me. "My father took that picture, Cady."

I stared at her, dumbfounded. "How do you know that?"

"The writing on the back of the photo. Those are his initials. The same initials are on all the photos in the files downstairs. My father took them all. He only ever kept one print. If someone wanted something printed off a negative, my dad would do it for ten or fifteen cents. But he never signed those ones. Never. So how did Beale end up with it?"

We looked at each other. I think we both knew the answer. Maggie's brief smile was followed by a long sigh.

"You think you know a person," she said. "Especially when it's a parent. But if there's one thing I've learned in my years on this earth, it's that kids know a lot less about their parents than they think they do. When you're a kid, you only notice certain things. I never knew that a man had been lynched in this town. No one ever talked about it. Now that I know what happened, I'm going to have to try to find out more. I have to find out what role my father played. I don't know that I want to know, but I need to know."

"I'm sorry, Maggie," I said.

She hugged me tightly.

"Send me your story when you've finished it. I want to read it. Promise?"

I promised.

The Justice Department agents drove me to the jail, where they said I could have a couple of minutes with Mr. Chisholm. They brought him into an interview room and handcuffed him to an iron ring attached to the table, which was bolted to the floor.

"What do you want?" Mr. Chisholm demanded. He spoke in a tone I imagined he used on his household help. "Come here to gloat, have you?"

I told myself that I wasn't sure what I wanted. But that wasn't true. I wanted to know.

My voice trembled when I finally asked my question: "Do you know who I am?"

Mr. Chisholm's lips curled into a sneer.

"She should have gotten rid of you. God knows that's what I wanted. And God knows I wish I'd made sure she did."

I forced myself to stay calm. I was going to say what I was going to say. There would be plenty of time to cry later, where he couldn't see me. Where no one could see me.

"Did they tell you who found the picture?" I asked.

"What picture?"

"The one that either you gave to Sheriff Beale or he found somewhere at the scene."

"I don't know what you're talking about."

But he did. It was in his eyes. Defiance. Not shame.

"LaSalle had it, didn't he?" I knew I was right.

"It was Nearing, the idiot!"

He meant Maggie's father.

"That Frenchie sweet-talked him into a trip down memory lane. Nearing claims he hadn't been drinking when he produced that picture for him, but if you ask me, that leaves him with no damn excuse for doing it at all."

"You told LaSalle you didn't want him around your daughter; he told you he had the picture. He was going to show it to Ellie, wasn't he?"

His face twisted with hatred. I thought he was going to spit at me.

"He asked me if Ellie really knew what kind of man she was living with."

"Everyone I talked to about her said she was sweet. She was nice. She must have been if you were so afraid of what was going to happen if she saw that picture, if she saw the smile on your face in it."

He stared at me, silent.

"You know what you did is wrong. And you didn't want her to know."

He dismissed me with a shake of his head.

"You turned out to be a troublemaker," he said. "You're just like your father."

I couldn't help it. I was proud.

ACKNOWLEDGMENTS

Many, many thanks to Teresa Toten and Eric Walters for taking the lead on the Secrets books and for inviting me along for the ride. A special thanks to Andrew Wooldridge for aiding and abetting the endeavor, and to Sarah Harvey, the series editor, whom I am beginning to think of as "long-suffering Sarah." And, of course, a shout-out to the other authors involved: Kelley Armstrong, Vicki Grant, Marthe Jocelyn and Kathy Kacer.

NORAH McCLINTOCK is the author of more than sixty YA novels, including books in Seven (the series) and The Seven Sequels, as well as two graphic novels. She lives in Toronto, Ontario. For more information, visit www.norahmcclintock.com.

Uncover more Secrets—
starting with this excerpt from:

A WEEK AGO

A week ago I lived in the Home. The Sevens, the Littles and the teachers were all the people I knew. I never really considered the rest of the world except in geography lessons or as settings for books.

A week ago I had never talked to a boy close up or bought my own clothes or tasted lemon meringue pie. I'd never met another brown teenager or seen anyone brown at all except on Joe's television.

A week ago I wouldn't have guessed I could get on a bus by myself or have a job interview without flubbing it or scrub a floor. I didn't know I even cared about who my mother was, let alone thought I might track her down like I'm a detective. I didn't know there were all these other parts of *me* tucked inside the Malou I'd been up till then.

That bus ride didn't just take me to a new place, it scraped off my outside and made me new too. It has only been a week since the fire, but it's as if I've travelled through time, hurtled forward and landed with a bump in a universe only half familiar. My space pod split open and here I am. All the qualities required to function in the new world are unfurling to reveal the new Malou, with wings and spikes and sharper taste buds, like it's part of evolution, only faster. A week instead of a millennium.

And who will I be another week from now?

NEXT DAY, AFTER WORK

Frankie is waiting for me outside the staff locker rooms at the end of my shift. It's his day off, so I get kind of warm-cheeked, pretty sure he's here on purpose to see me.

"Guided tour of Parry Sound begins in five minutes," he says in a funny announcer's voice. "Don't miss a single hot spot! Special discount for new arrivals includes supper at Bert's Beanery." He's talking fast and cocky.

Berna comes through the door behind me and takes one look at Frankie's flapping hands and sassy smile. She turns to me and raises her eyebrows. "You didn't need my help," she whispers. "You already got a nice fella."

Is that what they think? Is that what I hope? When I glance at Frankie, he winks.

"What's first?" I say. "On this world-famous tour?"

THE TOWER

We walk and walk and walk, uphill and away from the water.

"Where are we going?" I keep asking, because mostly we see only trees and a few little houses. But when we get there, wow, I know why he wanted me to see this.

An iron scaffold shoots straight up, as high as the sky, it looks like. Perched *waaay* up there on the top is a cute little white house, hexagon shaped, with a red roof and windows facing in every direction.

"I know the guy who lives here," says Frankie.

"Someone *lives* here?"

"Best pad in town," says Frankie. "Ray Shields. He had his appendix out a while back, and now we're buddies. Come on." Frankie heads for what I realize is a staircase. Flight after flight of steel steps go all the way to the top.

"We're, uh, going up there?"

"You're not scared of heights, are you?" He reaches out to take my hand, but I stay rooted for a moment.

How would I know if I'm afraid of heights? I never had the chance before to go higher than my room on the third floor of the Benevolent Home. Maybe I'm scared. Or maybe I'm a daredevil-in-waiting. Only one way to find out.

FROM THE TOP

Frankie's friend Ray has a rust-colored beard and the most astounding view from his windows, overlooking the Sound and the bay beyond, the town and a million trees. The trees are the reason for the tower. It is Ray's job to watch for forest fires all over the county and as far as he can see. He lets us look through the special binoculars, but he says when there's a fire, you don't even need them—you can see smoke puffing up like an arrow pointing to the trouble spot. I try to imagine what the Home looked like from up in the sky, a teeny flame like an ant's bonfire.

"Do you feel like an eagle, perched up here?" I ask.

Ray and Frankie laugh.

"Some days," says Ray. "For sure I wish for wings instead of having to use the stairs. But yeah, like with most beautiful things, the view is worth the climb."

We stand there looking out the windows for a long, long time. At the shivering treetops, at the way the water wrinkles, at dots of sails and spots of houses.

Then Frankie says, "I'm hungry."

SUPPER AT THE BEANERY

Whatever Bert's kitchen is offering, we can smell it before we get inside, spicy and tantalizing, its aroma wafting through the trees near the railway yards.

"There's no menu," says Frankie, opening the door for me like a gent in a movie. "You just eat whatever he's got in the pot."

Like in the Home, I think. Eat whatever's served.

It almost feels as if we're outdoors at a family picnic. There are so many windows, and people eat at long tables, sometimes right next to strangers. The iron stove to one side is enormous; Jumpin' Joe would be chartreuse with envy.

Frankie gets us plates full of beef stew and baked beans, swimming in gravy. "Save room for pie," he says.

But it tastes so good that I eat every bite and wish I could lick the plate. Frankie's done before me, grinning while I finish.

"Next time," he says, "you could come have supper at my house. My mama's a good cook too, but she cooks mostly Mexican food. You like *empanadas*? And *burritos*?" He makes the Spanish words sound...Spanish. He must speak it with his family, mysterious words that set him outside Parry Sound as much as his color.

"I don't know," I tell him. "I never ate anything foreign except that Chinese food."

He laughs. "*Foreign* is just a way of saying *not tried yet*. And not only food. You ready for pie?"

I hold my stomach. "Is it lemon meringue?"

"Cherry, I think." He picks up our plates. "Another few weeks and there'll be blueberry pie every day. That's my favorite. You see me, the end of July? I'm gonna have a big smile full of blue teeth."